Stalked

Cover Design: Designsbycharly

Editing: Susan Keillor

Proofreading: Haley Bottorff

Paperback ISBN: 979-8-9877506-7-4

Content Warning

Stalking behavior

Physical assault

Kidnapping

Murder

Graphic sexual scenes

Torture

Childhood trauma

Mention of Rape (off and on paper)

Tropes

Grumpy/sunshine

Gay awakening (more like Gabriel awakening)

Stalker romance

Hurt him and die

He falls first

Mafia

AUTHOR NOTE

While each book is a standalone, it is highly recommended to read in order.

This book follows along after Red Obsession in the Warpath series, only fifteen years later when Tobias from the first book and Gabriel from Red Obsession are grown up.

Blurb

Gabriel

I grew up being abused and hunted. It's nothing new to me.

But when my ex decides he needs to get rid of me because he thinks I know something about a suit man who keeps breaking into my apartment every night, everything turns upside down. I'm shoved back into the world of murder and torture. A place I declared I was never going to end up again.

Tobias

I grew up in the Mafia. In fact, I'm the Pakhan in America for my father. I'm a hard-ass, I'm silent, and I'm deadly.

But when I'm looking for the man that stole from me and find myself face to face with Gabriel, I can't help myself. I'm stalking him, staying in the shadows, unable to stop this obsession growing inside. Until someone touches what's mine.

And I do what I have to; I take him.

To those who want to be stalked and fucked like they're owned.

Same.

1

Tobias

Asurge of adrenaline courses through my veins as I take in the bloody mess hanging in front of me. I shove my hands in my pockets as I stare at Nathan, Billy's brother, hanging from the ceiling, blood dripping down to the concrete.

"Stop," his weak plea echoes around the dim warehouse. "I don't know... I don't know where he is. I don't know," Nathan rambles on, spit trailing down his chin, mixing with blood from the cuts Kyler gave him an hour ago. Unfortunately, I already know he has no idea where Billy is. If he did, he would've told us in the first ten minutes of Kyler working on him. But I can't let him go. That's not how this works. Not in our world. You either stay in it for life or you die.

Nathan and his brother Billy have worked for Derek, who works for me in the shipment of weapons. They thought they were stealing weapons from a small pool; little did they know that wasn't true. They were stealing from the Russian Mafia. Derek had a feeling Billy was doing something shady, and when Kyler followed Nathan, he found the siblings meeting with the cartel, Rafael to be exact.

No fucking trust in the damn Mafia.

"I know," I mutter, watching as the words filter through his head. Seconds later he finally realizes what I've said before his eyes snap to mine.

Dumb fuck.

"Please... Please, just let me go!" he screams, breaking out in a coughing fit. Probably from the broken ribs Kyler gave him. That's one thing that I enjoy about my best friend, Kyler. As much of a best friend as he is, he's also my enforcer. The one who enjoys the messier side of our lives, the physical part. Don't get me wrong, I enjoy the thrill of causing others pain, watching them bleed, ripping their organs out. But Kyler has a whole other side to him that thrives in this environment. He craves others' pain. For example, right now, he has that creepy smile, he can barely contain himself, and when he presses a palm against his junk, I know he's going to go to the club or one of our underground fight clubs after this. Not that I blame him. I wouldn't mind hitting a sex club after this, but it's not the same anymore. It's almost the same girls, the same fake tits and fake asses.

I'm just tired of that life.

Kyler throws his knife into the air, catching it blade first. *Fucking psycho.* Rolling my eyes, my laugh gets caught in my throat when Nathan cries even harder, mumbling something under his breath.

"I can't hear you. Speak up!" I growl, losing my patience.

"He...he has a boyfriend."

Kyler glances my way as if to say, *"Yeah right."* Because in our world you can't be gay, or bisexual. Granted, those aren't my views. I was raised by a wonderful mother who taught us that it doesn't matter who we love, as long as they treat us with respect and care for us. Nothing else matters. My father, on the other hand, I'm not sure how he feels about certain topics. Not that he ever would get a chance to disown me or my sister, Blake, for our preferences when it came to who we loved. My two aunts and mother would probably castrate him and bury him alive.

"I'll play along," Kyler finally says when I fail to say anything else. "Who's this boyfriend?"

"I don't kn–" Nathan screams, trying to curl his body inward. I hadn't even noticed Kyler moving, dragging the knife along his torso.

"I don't have time for your games. Who is this boyfriend!" Kyler hisses in his face.

"Gabe, Gabe something... I, he lives downtown near the art studio, Dreams something..." Nathan whimpers as Kyler drags the blade along his cheek. He doesn't break skin, but the thought is there.

Sending a text to Emilia to look into the owner of this art studio, Kyler paces back and forth in front of Nathan. I smile as Nathan flinches every time Kyler knocks into him, acting as though it was an accident. Thankfully, it takes Emilia less than a minute to text me back. Gabriel Hollow.

Nodding my head to Kyler, the psycho wastes no time, flicking his knife out, and plunging it into Nathan's throat. The psycho giggles, twisting the knife into his neck, watching the blood drain down his arm.

"Fuck..." Kyler sighs.

"Emilia sent me the address. I'm going to go check it out. You do...well, have fun." I chuckle, turning on my heel.

"You'll be safe?" Kyler asks, glancing over his shoulder.

"Always."

Walking out of the warehouse, I climb into my SUV and head back into town. I don't usually go out on my own. Being the head of the American side of the Russian Mafia puts a big red mark on your back. But for some gut-wrenching feeling, I want to see this Gabriel alone. I want to see who Billy supposedly is dating. I need to see who would be stupid enough to involve themselves in the Mafia willingly.

2

Gabriel

Something was clearly wrong with me. Being held captive should send me screaming for help, begging for them to let me go. Basically, doing anything but admiring my captor's hands as he flexed them by his sides. It was an odd thing to be fixated on, but something about his hands screamed at me. I wanted them wrapped around my throat, pressing against my chest, or touching my dick.

Preferably touching my dick, because the hard-on that I was sporting was not going to fix itself.

I really should not be thinking about this overly large man's hands, or what way he would take me. He's probably not even gay. In my experience, most attractive men aren't. Which is a shame because that's what I always seem to be attracted to.

Straight men. It's honestly a problem. Apparently, I never got the same gaydar most gays got. I have the straight-dar, or whatever you want to call it.

So, when he stepped towards me if I had to guess, he was around six foot three, his vibrant green eyes glued to my dull blue ones. My breath doesn't hitch from being frightened. I might get hurt or worse, die here. No, my breath hitches because all I can think about is opening the fly on this man's dress pants and sucking his cock down my throat. I bet he would be taken by surprise if I did that right now. He'd probably kill me, but at least I'd die with a cock in my mouth.

Something is seriously wrong with me.

"Imya," he mutters, not breaking eye contact with me. Frowning at him, I have no idea what he just said. Sighing, he drops down onto the coffee table across from me, the wood groaning when he puts all his weight down. His large thighs are on either side of mine. A faint hint of smoke and mint wraps around my nose. *Hmm, he smokes.* And though I don't normally find men who smoke attractive, this man is downright fucking hot. I can't deny that.

"Answer me," he demands, glaring his beautiful green eyes at me. He has somewhat of an accent, and though I can't tell, I know it's not American. I just can't pinpoint where it's from, and it's as though he's trying to hide it.

"What was your question?" I ask instead, twisting my fingers together. A nervous habit I got from my sister, Izel.

Rolling his eyes, I swear I hear him grind his molars together. He almost reminds me of Zion, my sister's husband. Zion, that fucker, is definitely not someone you want to mess with. He's a six-foot-seven monster, and I'm not joking. Zion is huge, and granted, I was a little scared of him when we first met. I like to think he's more like a teddy bear than Godzilla. But that's just me.

Suddenly, a hand wraps around my neck, pushing me back onto the couch. My eyes widen as this suit man towers over me. That hand that I so desperately wanted around my neck is now making my dick harder than possible. Call me a little fucked up, but whatever this man wants to do to me, I'm sure I'll let him. Just as long as I have a view of those delicious hands.

"I don't like repeating myself," he mutters. His accent comes out stronger and I'm even more intrigued.

"Where are you from?" I ask, unable to help myself. Licking my lips, his eyes travel down to my mouth before snapping back up to my eyes.

Cocking his head to the side, as if he's fighting with himself not to answer me, I squirm under his gaze, feeling unsettled in this awkward silence. But also holding onto a little hope that he doesn't look down between our bodies and take notice that my cock is hard.

"Otvet' mne, tvoye imya," he whispers so quietly that I almost miss what he says.

"I don't understand," I say, licking my lips, because, of course, they'd decided now is the time to become dry.

"Name, Little Rabbit," suit man whispers so gently, I'm not sure who it surprises—him or I.

I've played enough captive games to know I should never give into their demands. I claim to be smart and even claim that I know the best ways to get out of these situations. My sister is surely going to murder me, especially when I mumble, "Gabriel."

Something is wrong with me.

"Gabriel..." I shouldn't like the way he says my name, but I do, I really do. Releasing my throat, he steps back, eyes narrowed down at me. It's not until his phone starts to ring do I jump and release the breath I've been holding.

I need to get myself under control.

"Da," he snaps into the phone. Without breaking eye contact, he listens to the other person on the line. "Otvezi yego na sklad, ya za-konchu zdes'."

Again, I have no idea what he's saying. But the way he stares at me, speaking low into the phone... I squirm, my fingers locked together, my breathing uneven. I'm sure I'm about to die when he hangs up and pockets his phone.

Stepping over, he once again towers over me, and I lean back against the couch, trying to melt into it, needing to disappear. I flinch when he brings his hand up. The fear races around my head, clogging my throat. Suit man frowns, his eyes glancing between his hand that's still mid-reach, offended that I flinched from his actions. Seeming to come to some type of conclusion, he grabs my chin, dragging his thumb across my bottom lip. Surely straight men don't do this, not to other men, at least.

"Forget me, Little Rabbit," he whispers and before I can even question what he means, he backs away, slamming the door behind him, leaving me lying on the couch, confused and most of all turned on.

3

Tobias

I shouldn't have gone alone.

I should have made Kyler do this because even though I knew who he was. I still needed to make sure he was Gabriel, and now that I know, my bones ache, and my skin crawls. I feel like I'm hooked on drugs, and I need to see him again.

Which is why I'm standing outside his apartment door, my hand on the doorknob, fighting with myself. I shouldn't do this, I really shouldn't...

A small twist, and the door swings open.

Frowning, I take a single step back inside, knowing I shouldn't be breaking into his space again, but unable to now. I growl when I close the door behind me, trying to lock it just to find that the lock doesn't fucking work. Does he have no disregard for personal safety? Anyone, anyone worse than me, could just break in here and take him, or worse, kill him.

My feet move on their own, taking in his space that I never got to look at before. His apartment is shitty, and that's being nice. The couch that I had him pressed against sits against a wall that has seen better days. The off-white walls are cracked and, in the corner, the shitty wallpaper peels down. The dark coffee table sitting in front of the couch now has paintbrushes and half-painted canvas lying there. I'm surprised the table that's a piece of junk even held my weight earlier.

Stepping towards the corner of the living room, I snoop through the paintings. I'm not sure what I expected, but surely, it's not a bunch of death. It's the only way I can describe it, the feelings, the emotion Gabriel must have put in these. *What the fuck happened?* It's not until I get to the last one that the air leaves my lungs. I can't breathe.

In the middle sits a boy, different shades of black and gray. His arms hover over his face as he screams. The raw emotions, the pain and grief. It's unsettling, but I can't take my eyes off it.

Oh, Little Rabbit, what happened to you?

Soft snores reach my ears, stopping me in my tracks. Placing the artwork back in the corner, it doesn't take long to find his bedroom, with there only being two doors. Pushing the half-opened door, I'm hit with his smell, citrus, mint, and a hint of musk. I groan before I can stop myself. Refusing to even acknowledge the feelings I'm having towards another man.

I hold my breath as I make my way closer, praying that he doesn't wake up and find me hovering over him. I'm not sure what I would do. Gabriel lies on his back, his mouth slightly opened...fuck. Blood suddenly rushes to my cock, and the images of him on his knees taking my length filter into my head.

I wonder if he'd let me fuck his ass with no lube, or if he'd be a bitch and demand it. I could spit right on his hole, stretch him wide with my finger before I fuck his ass and own him. He'd look so beautiful on all fours, head on the mattress, ass in the air, spreading his cheeks apart as I take what I want.

Fuck, he'd look so good choking on my cock, turning different shades of purple as I fucked his mouth. No remorse. I wouldn't care if he couldn't breathe. He'd be a good boy and take my cock like the good slut that I know he is.

"Fuck," I hiss. I can't. I shouldn't, but my hand is already unzipping my dress pants, pulling my dick out. My hand wraps around my length, giving myself a good stroke before I'm already moments from cumming. I can't hold it. My balls swell, my vision blurs and I nearly fall when jets of cum shoot from my dick onto his face. "*Fuck, yeah.*" I moan, emptying myself onto his pale face.

Taking a deep breath, I bend down, grabbing one of his dirty shirts to wipe my hand and dick off. Tossing the soiled shirt back down, I tuck myself into my pants. My eyes are drawn to Gabriel's face, my cum seeping into his creamy skin. I can't help but spread my cum onto his lips, grinning when he sighs. Surprised he didn't wake up. I cock my head to the side. His blond hair tousled from sleep. And when his tongue darts out in his sleep, tasting me. I groan.

Hovering over him, my face mere inches from his own, I can smell his morning breath. Fuck. I could plunge my cock into his mouth, and he wouldn't be able to do a thing about it.

Gabriel turns away from me, pulling the covers to his shoulders. Sighing, I decide it's best if I leave now before I get hard again. Not that I can help it. He's damn magnetic, and I'm losing all control when it comes to him.

My phone vibrating in my pocket pulls me out of whatever trance I must be in. Pulling it out, Kyler's name flashes across my screen. Whatever it is must be important, so as much as I don't want to leave, not yet at least, I sigh, backing out of his bedroom.

"Da," I answer the moment I step out of his apartment, mentally reminding myself that I need to replace his lock.

"Situation at the club."

"What situation?" I growl, heading downstairs to my SUV.

"I killed someone," is all Kyler says before hanging up.

"Where've you been fucker?" Kyler chuckles the moment I step into the warehouse. Glaring over at him, I think about shooting him in his face as I lay my suit jacket on the table. For all intents and purposes, I wouldn't actually shoot him. At least not in the face. Maybe in the leg, something he could survive from.

"You good over there?" Kyler's voice broke through my thoughts. Snapping my head towards him, I nod. Refusing to acknowledge where I had been, he doesn't need to know that I'm secretly thinking of stalking Gabriel. The one man who can give us where Billy is, and the man I'm refusing to hurt for some unknown reason.

"Thought you said you killed someone?" I ask, nodding my head towards the man hanging from the ceiling. Déjà vu hits me, as we were literally just here a few hours ago.

"I did, and this fucker is next," he growls, shoving his knife into the guy's thigh. Whoever the poor fucker is screams, shaking his head, snot trailing down his upper lip.

"Care to explain what happened?"

"Just someone who thought he could take without asking," Kyler growls. The one thing about Kyler is that he hates liars and thieves. What am I saying? He hates everyone, honestly. He didn't grow up in a loving family like I did. His father was one of the soldiers Dad had. He was decent at his job, according to my Uncle Zane. But it wasn't until one day when I was ten that I walked in on Kyler's father, beating him and his mother. When his father punched me in the face and told me if I ever spoke a word of it to anyone, he'd kill me, I was scared. I mean, I was ten, and barely got the concept that my family was dangerous and other people would do anything to get their hands on one of the most dangerous Mafia leader's son.

Thankfully, Kyler ended up going to Zane and Salem, telling them exactly what happened. And when they saw the massive bruise on my cheek that couldn't be explained as just roughhousing, Aunt Salem gladly took that trash out, and he was never heard from again.

After that, Kyler promised he would always be there for me, and eventually, he became my enforcer and when I was sent to America, he came with me.

"That's unfortunate." I sigh.

"Where were you?" Kyler asks once again, stepping closer to me. That creepy fucking smile again is plastered across his face, and blood spots cover his neck and face.

"I went to Gabriel's apartment," I mutter, not making eye contact.

"And where is he?" he asks, his eyes glancing behind me. When I refuse to say anything, Kyler frowns, taking a wide step towards me. Now Kyler and I have never fought. Sure, we've spotted each other, but not once have we actually thrown hands at each other. The fucker would probably destroy me. He's got two inches on me, standing at six foot five. Besides being taller, he also works out and is more physical than me. I'm lankier and leaner.

"Tobias," Kyler hisses, narrowing his eyes at me. If he were anyone else, I'd shoot him.

"Don't '*Tobias*' me. Don't forget your place, Kyler." I hate pulling the *I'm the boss,* but he also doesn't need to stick his nose into my business. He has a habit of doing it, and usually, I don't care. But with Gabriel, I want him all to myself.

"Right."

Sighing, I shove my hands into my pockets. "We're not going to talk about it. This is like when you got your fist stuck in Molly's pu–"

"Fuck, okay, okay. I got it. No need to bring that nightmare up," Kyler growls, shaking his body to get rid of the bad memories. I chuckle, thinking back to that mishap.

"I broke into his apartment," I state.

"Yeah, that's usually what happens–"

"No, I mean I did it again. That's... that's where I was when you called. I went there after Nathan, and then I went back when he uh, when he was asleep." I can't look at him. We murder people all the time and torture them. But telling him that I broke into someone's apartment and watched them feels a little like crossing a line.

"Well, that's, that's different," Kyler finally says. Glancing over, he waits until we make eye contact to burst out laughing.

"Fuck you," I mutter. "Want to tell me what he did?" I deflect, hoping he takes the bait.

"Nice." Of course, he knew exactly what I was doing. "He was hurting one of the girls down at the club. Thought I'd take the trash out."

"Well, I'll leave you to it. Just text Emilia or Killian to wipe the camera feed," I say, making my way to the exit.

Climbing into my SUV, I fight the urge to drive to Gabriel's apartment once again, knowing this growing obsession can't go any further. That still doesn't stop me when I turn left towards downtown instead of right towards my house.

4

Tobias

One Month Later

The clouds block out the early sun, the fresh rain smell clinging to the air. My brows pull together, watching Gabriel as he steps out of his apartment building into the chilly air.

I wanted to get here before he woke up, but after having dropped Kyler off at his penthouse since he knew where I was going. I got here as quickly as I could, but it was fast enough.

Pulling my hood further down my face, I take a drag of my cigarette. Inhaling the smoke, I feel a moment of calmness. But it's lost the moment he takes a right and starts walking down the sidewalk. My blood heats as he keeps his head down, unaware of his surroundings. Why isn't he paying attention? The idea of something happening to him, because he's not paying attention, is irrational, but I'm barely holding on to any strength I have not to march behind Gabriel and simply kidnap him. To teach him a lesson. How can he be so fucking careless?

Taking one last drag from my cigarette, I drop it into a puddle before following behind Gabriel. Making sure to keep close enough that if someone were to try anything, I'd be there in an instant, but far enough that it doesn't appear that I am following him.

Shoving my hands into my pockets, I continue following Gabriel until he steps into Coffee Bears Co., the coffee place he always goes into and always comes out with an iced coffee, no matter the temperature it is outside, along with a bag. It took me a few days to figure out he got three donuts, one glazed, one with sprinkles, and one raspberry glazed. I only had to pay the barista a couple hundred to tell me.

Stepping inside, I stand off to the side, watching as he orders before stepping off to the side. His phone starts to ring. Flinching he quickly pulls it out of his pocket, answering.

"Hey," he mumbles, stepping further back. Closer to me.

Watching him from the corner of my eye, I try to keep myself up against the wall. I don't need any regulars or the same barista noticing me. Though it wouldn't be that big of an issue. I could just pay her off or *kill* her.

"Honey, you do realize Christmas is still two months away, right?" He chuckles into the phone. My gut turns at the word honey. I need to put a tracker on his phone. I want to see who he's texting and calling. I don't know why I haven't done it before. Probably because I don't want to get Emilia involved. But just like her mother, my Aunt Aziza,

Emilia is just as annoying but crazy smart when it comes to computers. Aunt Aziza and Uncle Killian, long-lost lovers, are too smart when it comes to hacking into systems and accounts. Emilia is just as bad. Might be even worse.

"I'll try to be there." He sighs, sounding sad and defeated. I didn't like that sound. "I can't make any promises. I have a job."

"Gabe!" the barista yells, setting his order down on the counter before walking away.

"Hey, listen honey, I'll see what I can do. But I have to go... yes, of course, love you too." Hanging up, Gabriel pockets his phone before grabbing his order and rushing out the door. Pulling my hood further down my face again, I step out into the cool air, once again following behind him.

5

Gabriel

I have a stalker.

That little shit might think I don't realize. But I know. I might not know who it is exactly, or why he continues to follow me. But I'm not as dumb as he thinks I am. If not for the white paintbrush with a black rose, he's left every single day for the past month, or my front door handle that used to be broken, never locking, and now magically is different and does lock, then it was the dry cum I had glued to my face when I woke up this morning.

It was disgusting, degrading, and downright fucking *hot*. Something was seriously wrong with me. There could be a million other things I'd like to be attracted to, but of course, for some reason, the suit guy and this stalker are my undoing. I don't know what I did to deserve this, but suit-man and stalker have been invading my dreams.

I blame it on my fucked-up childhood. I mean Dan, my father, isn't really my father. He's my uncle. My mother slept with my biological father, Dan's brother. Got pregnant with me and thought it would be a good idea to keep it a secret, only for it to come out that I wasn't Dan's. She was murdered. Along with my biological father, leaving me and my sister with a psycho who found it comical to beat me and let my sister-cousin be raped. It wasn't until I was fifteen and was almost raped myself that Izel and I got away.

That was fifteen years ago, and now, while my sister and her husband live peacefully in North Dakota, I decided to grow a set of my own balls and move to New York and teach art. I wouldn't say it's failing, but my apartment is, and I can barely afford to live. But it's all worth it to teach children to draw, to know that art is just as important as any sport out there.

Shaking my thoughts, I take a sip of my iced coffee. Turning the corner, I spot my art studio. I could still feel *him,* my stalker, close behind. I had to fight the urge to turn around and see if I could get a glimpse of him. I don't know how I could tell it was a guy and not a girl. Let's say I was trusting my gut, something I learned I had to do at a young age.

Pulling my keys out, I unlock my studio door, flicking the lights on before closing it and relocking the door. I might like that I have a stalker, but that doesn't mean I'm stupid and want something to actually happen to me.

Making my way into the back office, though, it's more like a closet. The whole studio is small, with two long tables along both walls, a large window next to the front door, and my office in the back corner.

It's small, but it's all mine. Sure, Zion and Izel paid for my schooling, and I'm grateful for their help, but now it's all on me to pay my way.

Setting my iced coffee down, I sit, pulling out the sprinkled donut. Shoving half of it into my mouth, I pull out my old laptop and start diving into emails.

It's not until a sharp knock at the door that I finally glance up from my artwork. Groaning, I glance over at the clock, frowning when I realize it's almost nine at night. *Fuck.* After reading the emails, I felt the need to paint, and I ate the other two donuts on the desk and began to work. I hadn't realized I was so wrapped up in my work until now.

"Gabe! I know you're in there. Open the fucking door!" Billy screams. Another row of heavy knocks causes me to flinch. I hate when I do that but call it PTSD or whatever you want. Loud noises, yelling, or fast movement do it for me.

Plus, Billy is a piece of shit. We barely dated for four months before we broke up. Finding him balls-deep in some girl in my apartment would do that. Not that I was all that surprised. He was out at all times of the night. I knew something shady was going on and should have trusted my gut. I still don't know what he was involved in, but I didn't want anything to do with him. So, I had no idea why he was here to begin with.

Rolling my shoulders, I make my way to the door. I should've ignored him and just went to the office. I'm not good at confrontation like my sister. I actually suck at it. It makes me uncomfortable, and nervous and usually causes panic attacks.

Taking a much-needed breath, I unlock the door and pull it open an inch. I don't need Billy barging in here. Who knows what he'll do? He's never physically hit me; he was more mentally abusive than anything.

"What do you want, Billy?" I ask, keeping myself halfway in front of the door.

"Let me in," he growls, stepping forward.

Shaking my head, I keep myself planted. Knowing all too well that if he truly wanted to get inside, there was no way I could stop him. I'm small compared to most men, and Billy is easily over six feet, and well over two hundred pounds. I'm short for a man, five foot seven, and usually I don't mind, that is until someone towers over me wanting to do harm.

"I'm working, I-I, just tell me what you need." My voice comes out small, and not as demanding as I try to make it.

"Just let me in, Gabriel!" He shoves his way inside, and my back slams against the wall. Billy throws the door closed, running his hand through his hair. I used to think it was hot when he did that. Now I just think he's ugly, in looks and personality.

"Well, you're in here. Now what?" I huff, crossing my arms over my chest. Hoping I looked more annoyed than scared. But for some reason, Billy being here, pulling on his hair...it was making me nervous.

"I need to know, I–fuck, I need to know if you told them anything," he nervously asks, glancing around the studio. Looking for what, I don't know.

"Tell who what?" I ask, furrowing my brows. I have no idea what he's talking about.

"I'm not stupid. I saw him at our apartment a few weeks ago."

"First off, it's my apartment," I hiss, no idea where this unfound anger came from. Maybe I haven't dealt with him cheating on me but fuck it. "Second off, I have no idea what you're talking about. No one ever came to *my* apartment, and–"

Suddenly Billy advances toward me, gripping my chin, and shoves me against the wall. "I saw him! I'M NOT FUCKING STUPID."

My vision blurs, the uneasy feeling that he's about to hurt me unsettling my stomach. I honestly have no idea what he's talking about, but I hate that he thinks he can just come in here and boss me around. And I hate even more that I'm letting him. That I'm bowing down and letting him put his disgusting hands on me.

"I saw him. I saw the fucking suit at the apartment!" he yells into my face. "I saw him, now tell me. What did he want, and what did you tell him?"

My breath hitches at the mention of suit man. While I do find him quite attractive, I never found out why he broke into the apartment, waited for an hour, and then left. Besides him questioning where Billy was and saying a little in another language, neither of us spoke. And I can't stop thinking about or jerking off to the thought of him.

Something is seriously wrong with me.

"I didn't tell him anything," I choke out, willing myself not to cry.

"I don't believe you!" he growls, hatred dripping from his voice. Well, fuck you too, buddy.

"Billy, I'm not lying." Even if I wanted to, I'm a shit liar, just like my sister. It's a fault, honestly. "He-he did ask, but I didn't know where you were. I couldn't even tell them, even if I wanted to." The words flew from my mouth, but they only seemed to enrage Billy more. His grip tightened against my jaw; I knew he was leaving bruises. "Billy please, stop," I plead. Suddenly, he shoves me harder into the wall, dropping his hand from my face.

"Tell them anything, you're dead. You fucking hear me!" he yells, not leaving a chance for me to say anything before slamming the door open and leaving me trembling against the wall, wondering what situation I just got tossed in.

Tobias

The moment I step inside the apartment door, Gabriel's snore reaches my ears. I smile at the sound. Knowing he's safe and asleep brings joy to my cold heart. I tried to get here before four in the morning, but while dealing with our missing shipments, I couldn't. As much as I didn't want to, I hated that I might have to use Emilia or Aunt Aziza to track Billy down. I know he has something to do with it. That little weasel was just a fucking drug runner and now he's running his own operation, with my fucking weapons. But it couldn't just be him. There's something else happening here. I just can't put my finger on it. It has to involve Rafael, there has to be a reason for the brothers' meeting with the cartel leader.

Closing the door, I glance around the apartment. His bag is thrown across the room, some of his artwork is smashed against the wall, and the paintbrush I left sits in the same place.

Something is wrong. Without thinking I tidy his living room up. Shoving the art books back into his bag, I place another white brush down, wondering where he's put the others. Has he thrown them away? Are they locked away somewhere? Surely, he knows someone is following him, breaking into his apartment. Why hasn't he called the police yet?

Shaking my head, I make my way into his room. Gabriel lies on his side, facing the door. I freeze for a moment when his snores stop. I don't know what I would do if he woke up and found me. Sure, I'm supposed to be the ruthless leader. I've killed plenty of people. I'm not supposed to be nervous. But I'd totally freak out. I'd have to kidnap him and keep him. I smirk at the idea. Kidnapping him wouldn't be the worst thing...

Thankfully, he starts snoring again, and my body slightly relaxes. My eyes search around his room, and just like the living room, it's trash. Yesterday it wasn't like this. Yesterday it was tidy and clean, everything had a home, but now it's almost as if a bomb went off. Clothes lay everywhere; art supplies were ripped apart. My eyes traveled over to Gabriel, willing myself not to wake him up and ask what happened and what was wrong. I don't have a reason for wanting to know. I don't know why I want to know so much about Gabriel. I just have this need. A need for him.

My legs carry me closer, my eyes traveling from his feet that peek out from his blanket all the way up to his face. His face.... Is that a fucking bruise?

What the fuck?

Peering down, I bend until I'm close enough to his face, too close for comfort. But I need to see if my eyes are just playing tricks on me. Sure enough, a clear thumb lays against the bottom of his cheek, along with finger bruises on the other side.

My breath comes in rough, the rage coursing through my veins. My hand's fist, my knuckles crack from the pressure. Who the fuck dare lay a hand on him? Who dares lay a hand on mine?

Whoa. That thought comes out of nowhere. And he can't be mine. Even if I have broken into his space multiple times a day for the past month. He's my dirty little secret.

But the pure rage I feel, this is different. I'm not the jealous type. I've never felt this pain, this... I haven't felt this type of feeling before. Dare I even say I care, and care more than just him being my friend?

Stepping back, I pace back and forth at the foot of his bed, my eyes unable to look away from his face. The questions swarm around, who hurt him? Why did they hurt him? I've watched Gabriel for the past month, and he never gave me the impression he was dating or seeing someone. He never goes anywhere but his art studio, that coffee shop, and the grocery store. He doesn't even have friends from what I understand.

Shit, I need to have Emilia put a clone on his phone. And a tracker. I need to know who he's talking to, and where he's going.

Taking one final look at Gabriel, I close his bedroom door. Taking my phone out, my finger hovers over Emilia's contact, debating on calling or texting her. I don't want to talk on the phone, so I text her instead that I need her to clone someone's number.

I don't get two feet towards the door before my phone starts vibrating, Emilia's name showing across the screen. I should've known better. Thankfully, I can still hear his snores, giving me the confidence to answer.

"I texted you for a reason," I growl into the phone, my eyes traveling to his bedroom door.

"If you need me to clone someone's phone, I need your phone near theirs."

That would make sense, though I don't know why she couldn't have just texted me that.

"Hello, you there?"

"Da, I… okay, hold on." Placing my phone down, as quietly as I can I go back into his room. His phone lies on the nightstand. Thankfully, I can ease it off the charger before I'm back in the living room and picking my phone up.

"Okay, I have it. What now?" I ask in Russian.

"Just open her phone and give me the number." I should correct her, but I don't. Instead, I do what she asks, giving his number to her. "Alright, now just lay both phones near each other. It'll take a few minutes."

I lay them down, standing there like a fool, questioning my own morals, I mean, I can kill someone. I'm in the damn Mafia. I'm not a good person. This feels wrong, but I also need to know. I need to know everything about him. Who does he talk to? Who was on the phone with him earlier? More importantly, who the fuck decided to put their hands on Gabriel? He's mine.

"Tobias?" Emilia's voice broke my thoughts.

"Da," I answer, picking my phone up and placing it against my ear.

"Dude, the Russian still?"

"Da."

"You're in America, shouldn't you, I don't know, speak English?" Emilia chuckles into the phone.

Rolling my eyes, I grind my molars together. Emilia is basically my cousin. Sure, her parents aren't related to mine, but her father, Killian, is the hacker for my father, while her mother is best friends with mine.

"Fine, don't say anything. I cloned her phone, you'll receive everything they receive, texts, notices of a phone call. I made sure there's no traceable information, so she won't have a clue something happened to her phone."

"Thanks," I say, hanging up and pocketing my phone. I need to get back to my penthouse before I search through his phone. I don't need to get wrapped up in snooping through his phone before he wakes up and finds me.

That would be a world of trouble I don't need right now.

Tobias

"Are you stalking him again tonight?" Kyler asks, shoving his workout clothes into the duffle. I swear this man literally lives at the fucking gym.

"I'm not stalking him," I grunt, taking a drag from my cigarette.

"Seriously, do you have to smoke in here?" Pulling his phone out, he begins typing something before saying, "Giving someone unwanted and obsessive attention. So, by Google's definition, you're stalking this fellow, Tobias." Grinning up at me like he won something, I feel the urge to shove my fist through his face.

Glaring over at my so-called friend, I can't help but hate that he's correct. In some sort of technicality, he's right. I just don't like to claim the fact that I might be, a hard *might be,* stalking Gabriel. But he also has to know, there's no way Gabriel doesn't know someone is stalking him. I leave a paintbrush every night. I even cleaned up his trashed apartment last night.

"So, are you?" Kyler asks again.

"I don't like that word," I huff, blowing smoke out from my cigarette.

"Yeah, well, I don't like you smoking in my penthouse, but yet here we are."

Rolling my eyes, I head to the bathroom, taking one last draw of my cigarette before flicking it into the toilet and flushing.

"Is that better?"

"Much. Now, back to the issue at hand. Why are you stalking him?"

Tilting my head, I lean against the doorframe. I truly don't know why I'm still stuck on him. I don't have a real reason. Just something about him spoke to me. He was barely nervous or scared when I broke in. He has yet to contact the police about that break-in or every night since.

"I don't have a reason," I finally answer.

"Don't have a reason, or don't want to tell me?"

"I don't have a reason," I lie again.

Kyler studies me for a minute before sighing and moving back towards his duffle.

"Where are you going?" I ask, realizing I don't have plans to leave the state whereas Kyler packs a bag like he is. Which is odd because he never leaves, not without me.

"Underground fight in an hour. I'm fighting against Tank," he mutters, refusing to make eye contact with me. Knowing Kyler, he has a reason for fighting against Tank, someone who works under us.

"You're going to be safe." It's not a question or even a statement, it's an order. Even if I don't like ordering him, I am his boss and nonetheless, his Pakhan.

Kyler snaps up, his spine ridged from my voice. He knows he can mess with me, we joke around, but that's all behind closed doors. In public, he's my soldier and listens to my orders.

"Yes, Pakhan." Kyler clears his throat, his arms immediately going behind his back. I hate the feeling I get when he stands like this, but I also love it. Knowing the simple change in my voice can make him or any of my men stand at attention and wait for my orders.

Holding eye contact for a minute later, I relax and nod my head at him. "Just text me when you make it out, *alive.*"

Kyler better make it out, but I also know when he gets in a certain headspace he can become a sort of villain, a monster if you will. He has a way of shutting out every ounce of emotion or feeling he has and destroying those around him. But if he needs this, then who am I to stop him?

"Okay, stand down or whatever." Waving a hand, I leave his bedroom.

"I'll text you; go have fun stalking your boyfriend." Kyler's laugh follows me out of his penthouse.

If only he knew the feelings I was having towards Gabriel.

Gabriel wasn't asleep in his bed when I got inside this time. Instead, he lies on the couch, his hand still firmly holding the pencil. Cocking my head to the side, I take in his shaggy blond hair, his long lashes feathered across his cheeks, and the faint dusting of hair on his upper lip. My cock begins to harden, trying to press my palm against myself. It does nothing but cause me to hiss. In doing so, Gabriel shifts, his eyes fluttering.

I should move, I should definitely move. Because just like before, I have no idea what I would even do if he were to wake up. I'd like to think he'd be more freaked out, but honestly, I'm sure I'd be the one having no idea what to do or what to even say. Thankfully, Gabriel shifts, rolling onto his side and dropping the pencil to the ground.

I can't help myself; I never can. Picking it up, I smile at the piece of paper that has fallen to the ground as well. It's a beautiful half butterfly that branches out to different kinds of flowers. There's no color, just shading and perfect. Fuck.

Taking the notebook, I place it on the table. Pulling the blanket from the back of his couch I lay it over his body. I don't have a reason for going to his room since he's not there, but I can't help myself. I've never been able to truly sneak around since he's always been asleep in here. But now I can. The moment I step inside, I'm hit with mint and citrus again. *His smell.* This does nothing to help my hard cock. No, it makes it worse. I try adjusting myself, but I know I won't get any real relief until I either shove my cock into his mouth or jerk off.

Ignoring my painful hard-on, I pull open the side table drawer, immediately finding the pile of paint brushes I've left. I don't have to count to know thirty-seven are in there. The drawer is filled and the smile across my face is rare, the warmth in my chest. It feels...nice.

Closing the drawer, I continue snooping around, pulling drawers open, finding his secret stash of candy and donuts in the other side table. Gabriel has a serious sugar addiction, worse than I've seen before. Worse than Aunt Salem who bakes all the goddamn time.

It's not until I reach his closet that suddenly his phone begins to blare. My skin breaks out in goosebumps, my spine ridged. And when I hear him fairly answer through the wall, do I realize I have very few options. Hide in the closet or under his bed, which from the looks of it, I won't fit. Or I can show him his stalker is here. *Yeah, that would not go over very well.*

Shoving myself into the closet, I leave it cracked just enough that I can see out but thankfully he can't see inside until he gets too close. And if he does, I'm fucked.

"Izel, it's three in the fucking morning!" Gabriel growls sleepily into the phone, walking into his room. He stops in the door frame, glancing around, his eyes skimming over the closet door.

I learned by going through his phone, that Izel is his sister. The one he calls honey, and much to my liking, she annoys him all the time.

"Yes, yes, I'm fine. I told you I'd let you know about Christmas, but like I've said before it's a few months away. I can't exactly just pick my life up and move back." Gabriel sighs, sitting on the edge of his bed. "Okay, Izel, calm down. Listen, it's too early, I have to be up in a few hours, and... Yes, Zion. See, even your husband is telling you to go back to sleep. Why are you awake anyway?"

I was wondering the same thing, but I couldn't speak on the matter. I'm the one hiding out in his closet because I'm too scared he'll find me.

"Well, on that note, I'm going to go...yeah, love you too." Gabriel hangs the phone up, tossing it somewhere on the bed.

Gabriel huffs, running a hand through his hair before he suddenly reaches under his bed pulling out a shoe box. I raise a brow. What does he have in there? But I don't have to wonder for long before he's pulling out... a blue dildo. Sure enough, Gabriel is pulling out the largest dildo I've seen. Nine or ten inches, a wide base, a slight curve at the tip.

Fuck, I need to get out of here. I need to somehow get past him and that... that thing in his hand before he...

I can't move my eyes. Not when he pulls his shirt off, leaving his bare chest out. His dusky, brown nipples scream for my mouth. I ignore the rational part of my brain that's screaming at me that this is all wrong. I'll deal with it later. Right now all I can do is watch him.

The moment he begins shucking off his pants, leaving himself naked on the edge of his bed, my own hands' cup my hardened cock in my pants. I know I shouldn't but when he reaches back into the box and grabs a bottle of lube, covering his fingers, I'm lost.

Gabriel leans back, pulling his legs up until his knees are against his chest. The room is so dark that I can barely see what he's doing. I'm almost desperate enough to move from the closet, but I can't.

My breath hitches, my eyes glued to his hand as he drags it back, my imagination running wild. It's almost like I can see it, his fingers rubbing against his hole, and the moment he groans, I know his finger is sinking inside.

Oh fuck.

My forehead falls against the doorframe, the closet door opening a little more than I like. But I can't stop, my zipper down, my cock in my hand. I spit into my hand before sliding over the tip of my cock, I moan low in my throat. I can't even find a fuck to care if he hears me. But Gabriel seems to be in his own little world, moaning himself. Precum leaks from my tip, and the moment he stops moving his finger inside himself, reaching for that blue dildo, I stop breathing altogether. When the tip of the dildo touches his hole, and slowly, ever so slowly, he begins working it in, pants and groans leaving his mouth, his head thrown back, I can only imagine what his face looks like. Gripping the doorframe, I force myself not to move forward. Instead, I fuck into my hand, watching as he moves the dildo in and out.

My hand moves vigorously; the pressure nearly starts to become too much. But I can't cum. I need Gabriel; I need *him* to cum first. I don't have to wait for long. Gabriel moans long and loud, cum spurting from his dick, landing somewhere, somewhere I can't see. My vision blurs, my chest heaves as cum shoots into my hand, some landing on the door and floor.

"Holy fuck." Gabriel laughs, dropping the dildo onto the floor, his legs stretching out. I watch carefully as his breathing slowly returns to normal, and two seconds later his snores fill the room. I chuckle, and bending to grab something off the floor, I wipe myself clean. Taking a risk, I leave his closet.

Tiptoeing closer, I pick the dildo up. It's warm and slippery and the urge to shove it back into his hole blinds me. Gripping the base, I step forward peering down over at Gabriel, his mouth opened, his snores loud and... fuck.

I force myself to step back, all the way back until I'm in the bathroom. Closing the door, I drop the toy into the sink, running water and soap over it. I have no idea if I'm doing this right, or if soap is even right to clean this thing with. I mean, it should be. It's soap; soap cleans well enough.

Opening the cabinet, I find a towel. Drying it off, I make my way back into his room. Gabriel is still in the same position. Dropping the dildo into the shoebox with the bottle of lube, I place the box back under his bed. Using the towel, I'm still holding onto, I debate on wanting to wipe the cum from his chest and stomach but decided not to so I don't wake him up. Trying my hardest to not peek down at his cock, I fail. His dick is soft, laying against his leg, cum dripping from his tip down onto his thigh. The urge to bend down, swallow him whole, to get his dick hard again is blinding.

Shaking my head, I grab the blanket from the corner of his bed, pulling it up and over him.

I know I shouldn't, yet I'm a sucker for Gabriel. Bending down I press my lips against his forehead, ignoring the warmth that claws at my chest, tightening around my heart.

I need to get out of here, right now, but first I grab the same paintbrush from my back pocket and place it next to his phone.

He'll be mine soon—soon enough.

Kyler stands behind me, with a fresh bruise and a split lip. The bags under his eyes tell me he hasn't been to sleep yet, but that's his own damn fault. Though I can't say much—I haven't either. After leaving Gabriel's apartment, Emilia called saying she had details on Billy's whereabouts, which brings us to now. Sitting across from Antonio and his son Maddox, the Italian Mafia, who from Emilia says has been keeping tabs on Billy.

"It's lovely to see you again, Mr. Volkov. I wish it were under better circumstances. What was the reason again?" Antonio grins over at us. Gritting my teeth, I refuse to take the bait he's trying to wave in our faces.

Ever since I was little, I overheard Salem and her hatred for the Italians. No matter who came into power, it was always 'fuck them'. Granted, it was for good reason. Antonio gets on all of our nerves, but he came into power after Salem killed Luca. Antonio is some long lost brother of Luca, and a whole other story.

"Billy," is all I say, taking a sip of my whiskey.

"Ah, yes, this Billy." Antonio chuckles, nudging his son, who looks seconds from murdering all of us on the spot. Not sure who pissed in his cheerios, but he needs to reel it in before Kyler knocks him down from his pedestal.

"I need his location."

Biting my cheek, I hold their stares as Antonio mulls over whatever is going on in his tiny brain. I swear he does this shit on purpose, and there is nothing I hate more than people who waste my time, especially when they already knew the answer.

"I need something from you first... let's talk about Salem Gray."

My eye twitches, knowing this isn't going to end well. Many have tried to take her out, only they end up six feet in the ground.

7

Gabriel

Thirty-nine paint brushes.

That's how many my stalker has left behind. I should be completely freaked out, especially after this morning when I woke up to find not only my blanket covering me, but multiple other things didn't add up.

I fell asleep after having the most mind-blowing orgasm of my life. That blue dildo, my absolute favorite one, felt so good. Thinking about the suit man, thinking what he would do if he found me spread out on the bed. I swore I heard someone grunting along with me, but before I could even clean myself up, I fell asleep. That post-nut clarity sure does hit differently.

When I woke up a few hours later, my cum was dried to my chest and stomach, the blanket covering me. The oddest thing though, my favorite toy wasn't on the floor where I knew I'd dropped it. No, instead it was cleaned and back in the shoebox under my bed. And that same white paint brush next to my phone.

I shouldn't like it. I really shouldn't. But fuck did I.

A loud bang breaks me from my thoughts. I don't have time to look up before I'm shoved against the table, my side hitting the corner. I scream out in agony only to have a fist plowed into my face. My head snaps back, pain exploding everywhere. My knees give out, crumpling to the floor, my vision blurry. I can feel the blood drip from my nose.

I need to get up. But I can't, my legs feel too heavy to carry my weight.

"I told you I wasn't stupid." *Oh, oh fuck.* What is Billy doing here? And most of all, why is Billy punching me? "You know I saw him. I saw him leave your apartment this morning."

What is he talking about? Who is he talking about?

I try to scoot back, try to do anything, but I don't get two feet before he kicks my stomach. Not stopping there, he kicks my side, my ribs screaming.

"Stop! Ohmygod, *please* just stop," I cry out, my arms wrapping around my stomach, pleading for this to all stop. I can't go through this again, I can't.

"The thing is, Gabriel, you lied to me. I saw him leaving your apartment. I know you told him something and I want to know what you told him."

"Who?" I yell, my arms holding my stomach as if that's the only thing keeping me grounded.

"The fucking suit! Who else do you think I'm talking about?" he screams, kicking me in the back once more. I grunt from the force, crying out in pain again. "I told you! I fucking told you if you said anything I was going to kill you. I told you! Now, I'm going to fucking murder you!"

His boot connects with my face; pain explodes behind my eyes. My limbs lock up, unable to do anything. I can feel the blood dripping down my face, blood coating my tongue.

"I should've known you couldn't keep your damn mouth shut," he growls, and another round of kicks hit my face and stomach.

I don't know how long I lay like that, him hitting me. I scream and plead with him to stop. I can't take this much longer.

I'm dying.

Tobias

Fucking Antonio. The balls on that guy, thinking I would just give up where my aunt lives. Little does he know Salem is already watching his every move. Like I said, she doesn't trust the Italian, and I guess we shouldn't either. Between trying to find Billy, that fucking rat that's been stealing my damn containers of weapons, figuring out how to get close to Gabriel without sounding like a complete stalker, and now having to deal with the Italian, along with the cartel that was making a deal with Billy and Nathan, it never fucking ends.

But first I can see Gabriel. Just to make sure he's okay, and breathing.

Pulling up a block from Gabriel's art studio, I climb outside, checking my phone once more making sure he's still there. Sure enough, he is. Pulling out a cigarette from my suit jacket, I relax the moment I inhale the nicotine.

My feet eat up the sidewalk leading to the studio. It's not until I'm near the door that I hear someone grunt. A muffled scream, and then something breaking. Throwing my cigarette down, I shove my weight against the door. Thankfully, the old door is nothing and breaks easily. My eyes drop down to Gabriel. I only know it's him because his shaggy blond hair is a mess, blood covering his entire face. The fury I feel ignites, zeroing in on the fucker that's standing above him.

Billy.

"Fuck," he gasps, backing away from Gabriel. My little rabbit. *Mine.*

I don't give Billy time; I pull my gun out from my holster and shoot him between the eyes. He doesn't deserve a quick easy death, but one glance down at Gabriel, and I see he doesn't look good. Yanking my phone up, I dial Kyler as I kneel down next to Gabriel.

"Da," he answers, breathing heavily.

"I need help," I whisper, my heart beating too fast for my liking. I'm normally good in these situations. But I can't breathe. Everything in me freezes and it feels as though I've been hit by a semi.

"Location," Kyler snaps, turning more serious than he was seconds ago.

"His studio." I take a deep breath, hating that I press two fingers to his neck. Checking his pulse, I wait and continue to wait. It's faint but I can't move my hand away. I can't. I need to make sure he's still alive.

What feels like hours later, heavy footsteps fill the front of the art studio.

"Tobias?" Kyler's voice fills the empty space. "Shit, what happened?" he asks, kneeling beside me.

"Billy," I growl. I don't take my eyes off Gabriel, knowing if I do, if I look at Billy, my restraint will break and I'm barely holding on.

"He alive?"

"Barely," I whisper.

"Alright, come on. Let's get him to the house. I'll call the doctor to meet us and call the clean-up crew to take care of him." Kyler is talking and walking, moving faster than myself. I don't know what is wrong with me, but I can't focus. I can't focus on anything but the look of Gabriel's bloody face. His breath comes in short and labored.

"Tobias!" Kyler yells, snapping me into action. Wrapping an arm around Gabriels' back and legs I lift, carrying him outside to Kyler's truck, praying to a God that I wasn't sure if I believed in or not, but praying he saved Gabriel.

8

Gabriel

My head is going to explode at any minute. I can barely open my eyes, and squinting only makes the pain worse. I groan, settling my head back onto the pillow. The memories of Billy breaking into my art studio flood back. Him punching me, getting kicked over and over again. The begging and pleading that he would stop, only my ex didn't. No, he continued hurting me. The pain was unbearable. I passed out.

I vaguely remember the gunshot, the voices. I don't know who it was, they merge together with the splitting headache I have. But I remember them. Both men, both saved me, somehow.

Just as I think about trying to open my eyes again, a door opens and closes. Two sets of heavy footsteps fill the silent room. My body tenses, not knowing what to expect.

"Damn, he's still asleep?" one of the men says.

"I had the doctor give him something to put him to sleep." That voice is so familiar, I just can't place it.

"Interesting, well now that he's here... what do you plan on doing with him?" That's a very good question. One I would like to know as well.

Only the other, the familiar voice doesn't say anything.

"To–"

"Shush," he growls, causing the other to stop talking. I frown, wanting his name.

"Do you... do you know why Billy was there beating the shit out of him?" the less angry one asks.

"No," the angry one grunts.

I don't like this conversation. I don't want to be a part of any of this. I should have never dated Billy; I knew he was trouble from the beginning. And when he threatened me, I should have told Zion. Zion definitely would have made sure they never found his body again.

"Have Emilia look into him; I want to know everything there is to know," the angry one orders, not long before the door opens and closes once more. I can't explain the feeling, but I know he's still here. But the feeling is different from a moment ago. My body was on edge, confused, but now, I feel safe. The same feeling when I woke up to find a paint brush, to find my apartment cleaned after Billy first hit me and I had trashed it.

It's him.

"I know you're awake." His thick accent is there. It's clear, better than the day before. Russian, and fuck he sounds so damn hot.

Peeling my eyes open, I sigh in relief when not only are the blinds down, and not much sunlight comes in, but that my head isn't pounding as hard as it was when I first woke up.

Only when I finally take in my surroundings, I'm hit with that same mint and smoke smell. His hair is styled and slicked back. The suit he always seems to wear fits him well. God, he is just as hot as he was then, only now I'm not feeling nervous or scared. I feel drawn to him, and my cock definitely takes notice of his hands again. The one I still want wrapped around my throat.

"How do you know Billy?" he asks, his voice demanding and I'm weak. I'm so weak when it comes to men, especially this man. But what will he think of me when I tell him that Billy was my ex?

I must have been quiet for too long because the brush of his thumb against my skin, let alone my cheek, causes too many reactions. First and foremost, I hiss, the pain to my face, but also my cock likes his touch and aches for more. Just a little more south.

"YA ne lyublyu povtoryat'sya, no, kazhetsya, ya ne mogu sderzhat'sya, kogda delo kasayetsya tebya."

I'm shaking my head the moment he starts speaking. I don't understand what he's saying.

"How do you know Billy, Little Rabbit?"

His thumb hasn't left my cheek, the cool sensation oddly feeling nice, a shiver cascading down my back.

"He's my ex," I whisper.

His face scrunches up, a look of pure disgust. *Why does he look like that?*

"I don't like the sound of that." I'm not sure who is more shocked, him or me. My eyes widen at the same time his does. Only he's quicker to recover, whereas I'm shocked to my toes in what he said, just not understanding what he's saying.

"Has he hit you before?"

"No," I immediately answer, before I realize that's not quite true. "One time."

"One time?" Oops, he's back to being angry, only it's at me. And I do not do well with men who get angry. I do the opposite, the total and complete opposite. I shut down, I get flashbacks, and shit... I don't like this feeling, not one....

"You hear that!" Dan screams at me, laughing in my face. The sounds of my sister's screams echo around the small hallway. I might be ten, I might be a child. But I know what they're doing. I know what is happening. And no matter how much she begs or that I beg, they laugh. We're jokes to them.

"It's all your fucking fault! It was you! You're the one who keyed the bike!" Dan yells once more just before Izel screams at the top of her lungs begging them to stop.

"I–we, no we didn't. I–didn't do anything!" I cry, fisting my hands at my side, hating myself for being born, hating that I'm the reason she's going through all this. I didn't ask to be born. I didn't ask our mother to cheat on Dan, to get pregnant. I didn't ask for any of this.

"It's your fault I'm so fucking angry!"

"Shhh, come on, Little Rabbit." That accent floats back to me, bringing me back. Heavy breaths reach my ear, wondering who's breathing so heavy, only to realize it's me. I'm the one who's breathing so hard. "That's it, come back," he coos, the cool touch of his hand brushing my hair from my face.

"I–I'm sorry," I croak out, hating the break in my voice. And hating even more he's witnessing my panic attack. Izel and Zion are the only ones who see them, and usually it's Izel who has to bring me back.

"Don't apologize." His voice once again sounds angry, and I can't afford to have another flashback. I can't, not with him right here.

"Billy," I mumble, trying to go back to our previous conversation.

He growls again, and I grit my teeth.

"Yes, him. He's only hit me once, once before..."

He drops his hand from my face, biting his cheek. Nodding his head, he doesn't say anything, just reaches for the door.

"Are you at least going to tell me where we are!" I yell at the back of his stupid head.

"In my home," he says, barely sparing me a second glance.

"Oh yes, thank you, glad we cleared that up." I hiss through my teeth. I thought dealing with Zion was a bitch and a half. No, this suit fucker brings short answers to a whole new meaning. "Care to explain where exactly your *home* is?" I ask, tightening my jaw only to let go a second later when the pain shoots through my neck.

"Not really." He shrugs, fucking shrugs like it's no big deal, now that I'm realizing I'm inside a stranger's house.

"Well, I care, so tell me."

He seems to think about it for a minute before finally looking back at me. I'm hopeful he's going to tell me, only to quickly die when he says, "I can't tell you."

"What the hell do you mean you... You can't tell me? What does that mean?" My voice rises, irritation clawing at my throat. How dare he? Even if he is hot, and so fucking sexy standing there. He has absolutely no right.

A sharp knock on the door stops him from answering, not that he was going to tell me anyhow. "Come in," he says instead, earning a glare from me.

"Pakhan Dmitriy, razgovarivayet po telefonu," someone says into the barely opened door. Angry one mutters something in the same language before the door is closed, and he's looking back at me. *Down boy, he's not looking at you,* I tell my cock, because the way he's perking up, might as well call me a cum slut. I bite my lip instantly, trying to hold my groan in but it's too late.

"Gabriel..." Tobias mumbles, running his hand down his face. "Did you just–"

"We're not talking about it. I don't even know your name, and you haven't answered me where we are. *Andddddd,* before you say '*my house*'" I say trying to drop my voice down to match his and failing, "I'm talking about what state, how long have I been out? All the questions. You know I have a sister that's going to wonder where I'm at if I don't answer her million questions she texts me," I huff, ignoring the gaze of my kidnapper.

Suddenly his hand is wrapped around my throat, our noses an inch apart. "You'd be mindful of how you speak to me. I don't take kindly to–"

"I don't do well when people raise their voices at me or when they're mad at me. Especially men." I have no idea where that came from, but I felt like it needed to be said. And from the conflict echoing around the suit man's face, I'm not sure how he's taking it either.

Nodding his head he whispers, "I'll be mindful of your needs." Brushing his thumb across my lips, I have all of two seconds before he's backing out of the room and closing the door softly behind him.

I might have been kidnapped, but that didn't mean I was just going to sit around and be a sucker in bed. Suit man can just go straight to hell; he had no reason to take me. However, I'm grateful because, from the little memory that I *do* have, the suit man ended up saving me from Billy.

I shiver from the thought of Billy, the way he so easily beat the shit out of me. Just because he thought I told the suit man where he was. I had no idea where Billy was, nor did I care. The moment I found him cheating on me, he was forgotten, or rather I wanted to forget about him.

Tossing the blanket off me the best I can with a bruised and broken body, I ignore my surroundings, heading straight to the bathroom across the bed. I might be able to feel the wreckage of my body, but I needed to see it. I needed to see what Billy had done and what the suit man had seen.

Flicking the light on, I'm blinded for a moment from the fluorescent lighting. When they finally adjust, I'm shocked at what I see. I sigh. My left eye is swollen and heavily bruised, and my nose must have been broken. There are deep purple and black bruises riding along my nose down my right cheek. My forehead even has a damn bruise. Dry blood coats my hairline. Some of it appears to have been wiped from my hair. Though I'm no longer blond in some areas, I'm a damn redhead. Along with a bird's nest that rests on top of my head.

Taking a deep breath, I shuck off my clothes, ignoring the fact that I wasn't wearing these sweatpants or the gray shirt when I was attacked. My eyes zero in on the colorful scattered bruises across my ribs, and stomach. Fuck, Billy really did a number on me. And worst of all, the clear outline of his fucking boot is now imprinted on my damn shoulder.

Gritting my teeth, I narrow my eyes in the mirror. Fuck Billy. Fuck suit man and fuck this fucked up shit.

Breaking my stare, I turn towards the shower, lukewarm. I'll never understand women and their hot showers. I've seen how red Izel's face is after her shower—a tomato. It's so red, I'm surprised she hasn't actually burned her skin.

By the time I'm done washing and putting the clothes that are *definitely* not mine, my body is exhausted. Opening the bathroom door, I finally take in the room. Dark gray walls and for the most part the room is kind of depressing. To the left of the bed are French windows, black curtains pulled back letting in the sunlight. Unfortunately, nothing else besides the bed, side tables, and dresser.

Sighing, I glance at the door suit man left from, debating on if I should risk walking out. Maybe no one will be on the other side. Or there could be a whole cavalry outside ready to murder me.

Suddenly the door opens. I tense, realizing that's exactly what could happen. Only it's not a team here to kill me. Instead, an older woman steps in holding a tray of some sort.

"Oh...uh, hello." She smiles up at me.

My mouth waters when I zero in on the tall glass of I'm assuming orange juice.

"Hello, not to be rude. But is that orange juice?" I ask, stepping forward, twisting my fingers together.

"Uh, yes, sir," she shyly says.

"No need to say, sir," I say, waving her off. "But if you don't mind, I would love that juice. I'm thirsty and, oh shit is that pancakes?" I nearly moan at the sight, my stomach growling on cue.

"Yes si– Uh, yes." Side-stepping me, she places the tray down on the dresser, her eyes darting everywhere but at me.

"Am I making you nervous?"

Shaking her head, she's still unable to meet my eye. I don't like that, I really don't. I'm not used to others feeling uncomfortable around me. Granted, I don't like dealing with people. They make me nervous. Blame it on my past but being around people, it's weird and odd. I can be around younger kids; they aren't aware of the hurt that I've been through. But most men are taller than me, and then women act as if something is wrong with you when you turn down their advances.

"What's your name?" I finally ask, realizing I'm staring at her.

"Amy," she mumbles.

"Well, hello Amy, I'm Gabriel." Holding my hand out, I wait for Amy to take it. What feels like minutes later, she reaches over, slipping her hand in mine. She barely shakes my hand before dropping it like she's on fire. Rolling my eyes, I nearly limp toward the orange juice and pancakes.

"Well, now that we've officially met, any way you can..." I don't get to finish my sentence before Amy runs out of the room, literally running, slamming the door as she goes. "Well, fuck." I sigh, shoving a bite of pancake into my mouth.

Chewing angrily, I can't help but be bothered by the fact that not only did the suit man apparently save me, but he also walked off before I could even tell him who Billy was, and he couldn't even tell me where we were. Sure, at his house, but where was his house? Also knowing Izel, the moment she can't get in contact with me she's going to tell Zion who's going to tell Killian, who's going to tell Aziza. Sure, Killian is a very skilled hacker for one of the Mafias out there. But Aziza is much better. She was the one who found my sister when Dan kidnapped her years ago.

Aziza will find me. I only hope it's sooner rather than later.

9

Tobias

"Are you out of your fucking mind?" Kyler yells at me for the millionth time.

Sitting back in my office chair, I can't even pretend to not know what he's talking about. But I also can't bring a single fuck to care about his opinion. Granted, I care. I do care for Kyler. But I just don't care what he thinks about this.

"Tobias!" Kyler growls, placing his hands on my desk, trying his best to get my attention.

"Hmm?" I hum. Playing dumb seems like the best choice, and I can do that well. Somewhat anyway. Maybe not all that well with Kyler.

"Knock it off."

"What's your problem now?" I sigh, sitting back.

"You brought him here? You brought him here! Why, why on earth would you do that?"

The urge to protect Gabriel was overwhelming. It was none of his business who I brought to the penthouse or my home out of the city. It was no one's business but mine. Gabriel is no one else's business. No one's but mine.

Mine.

"Tobias, you're ignoring me. I don't like being ignored." Kyler sighs, stepping away from my desk.

"I'm not ignoring you."

"You are. You've got that look on your face, that look when you're feeling angry. Which I don't understand. Why are you angry? It can't be at me, and it can't be your father. He just said he's going to handle Antonio and Salem's situation. Which is wild because surely Salem can handle herself."

"I don't have a reason, I just..." What the fuck am I supposed to say? I'm feeling things for a guy, and I'm pretty sure that I'm bisexual. I have no idea how my family, mostly my father, would handle this. Men in the Mafia are supposed to marry women. Usually it's set up, nonetheless. Men marry women in the Mafia. Mind the fact that my father saved my mother and married her. Besides that it's very uncommon.

"Just what?" Kyler breaks the silence.

Shaking my head, I refuse to think about my personal issue at hand. Instead focusing on the missing containers and what Billy did with them.

"Have they found anything in Billy's apartment?" I ask.

"Billy doesn't have an apartment, or anywhere to live for that matter. The only location we've found him living in was Gabriel's place. And from my understanding since you've been breaking in there every–"

"Watch it, Kyler," I snap, pointing my finger at him. I might be his best friend, but he still needs to respect me.

"No, there's nothing that has been found."

"Have Killian look into Billy some more. Maybe there's someone closer to him that we don't know about."

"On it," he murmurs.

"Great, so it's settled. I'll get word out soon about different locations." Kyler smiles, getting to his feet.

"Great," I mumble.

"I'm going to grab something to eat and then head out. You need anything?"

Shaking my head, Kyler is out of the office. I pull the computer feed up of Gabriel's bedroom, just in time to watch Amy, the older lady I hired when I found her sleeping on the street. Once I got her set up in the guest house a mile behind this house, she quickly learned the ropes and never looked back.

Amy is quiet and timid, but Gabriel is outspoken with her. I love it. I can't explain why my body reacts to him; it just does. From the moment I stepped foot in his space, everything shot to the surface. His smell was intoxicating, his artwork was everywhere, and the way he snores loudly.

My eyes are glued to the screen, watching as he shoves pancakes into his mouth, then downs the rest of the orange juice. I thought four pancakes, a tall glass of juice, and a banana would be enough, but the dude downs everything within five minutes. Cleaning the plate off.

Wonder what he would look like choking on my cock.

I groan at the thought. I shouldn't want him. But I do.

I really fucking do.

My mother oughta beat my ass.

I was surely raised better than this. Even if I was raised to murder and hurt others, I was raised as a gentleman. Mom made sure of it. You open doors for others, especially women. You walk on the outer side of the sidewalk. The whole ordeal. Mom wasn't raised like Dad. She lived in a small town in Ohio. Granted, she was kidnapped when she was twenty and then sold and rekidnapped by Dad. But never mind that—she was raised right, and in doing so raised me and my sister just the same.

If I wasn't going to Hell for the wrongdoing I've done before, I'm surely going to Hell for this.

Gabriel's snores fill the bedroom, his arms thrown over his face, the blanket halfway off, leaving his bare chest on display. His dusky pink nipple causes my mouth to water, and blood rushes to my cock, hardening at the sight.

I shouldn't.

But I'm already going to Hell.

Unzipping my dress pants, I tug my pants down enough to release my cock. Hissing at contact, spitting into my hand I give myself a slow tug before running my thumb over the tip. Precum leaks from my tip. I try to stay silent as I stroke myself. But the sight of him, fuck.

Gabriel rolls onto his stomach, leaving his boxer-covered ass on display. It wouldn't be that hard to just pull them down. I've never had sex with another man before, but I imagine it's not that hard.

"Fuck," I hiss, my balls drawing up. I shouldn't be doing this, but it's too late to stop. My eyes slam shut, my cum shooting out onto his back. My breaths come out uneven, and though I do feel much better, I now realize he's going to know who came on him last time.

10

Gabriel

The nerve of that guy. The *damn* nerve on suit man, thinking he can just come in here, jerk off, and leave his cum all over me?

What a fool. Of course, all along it's been the suit man breaking in—it's the only thing that makes sense. I'm not sure why I thought it was someone else, but of course, it's him. The one who broke in came on my cheek a few weeks ago and has been leaving those paintbrushes. I'm such a damn fool.

But if it's not him, then I have another stalker out there. One too many stalkers at that.

But damn him for thinking he could just come in here, even if it is his house. Or so I'm assuming. And to just jack off and cum on me, and without even getting me off.

Which is why as soon as he leaves the room, I shower. Granted, I had to take care of myself first. I don't think I ever got hard so quickly or came within seconds of touching myself.

Now I'm sneaking around the house like I'm the one who's breaking into his space. The first thing I notice is that the guy is obsessed with everything dark. The walls are black, the curtains are black, and the damn floors are dark enough that they might as well be black too. Seriously, what's with this place? Why is it so hard to have some light, some art?

Following the hallway, everything is emotionless and bland. It shouldn't bother me; I'm not staying here. But no one should live like this. It's too weird, too empty. No one should live here. Not even my worst enemy. Actually, that's a lie. I want him to rot.

At the end of the hall, I'm surprised when I step foot into a large open space. To the left holds a decent-sized kitchen, an island with four barstools. And to the right is a sectional couch and a TV above a fireplace. Across is another hallway that's calling my name.

I probably already overstepped, but then again if he didn't want me walking around, he should've locked the door. Shrugging my shoulders, I bypass the living room and kitchen. The living room is more enticing anyway.

Doors line up against the hallway, but I don't stop until I reach the one at the end. The light shines from beneath the door, and the more nervous I get about opening it the more I want to. I just can't leave things alone; it's been an issue since I was a child. It's probably the reason I got beat so much.

My hand reaches for the doorknob. *I shouldn't do this, I really shouldn't… I can't.* I twist the handle, pushing it open. My eyes are immediately drawn to a set of large French windows, going from wall to wall. A dark oak desk sets in front looking towards the door. It's plain, nothing but a small stack of papers, a pen, and a simple laptop.

God, why is he so damn boring?

Glancing to my left, a sectional, a coffee table, and a small bookshelf sits. Simple and again, so boring. The walls are dark gray, the floor the same dark wood the rest of the house is. For fucks sake I need to talk to his interior designer because first they did a shit job and second, they surely need to be fired.

Stepping further in, my hand reaches towards the desk, feeling the wood against my fingertips. I don't know much about real wood or fake wood, but this definitely feels real. My eyes snag to the folder that lies on top of the stack of paper. *"Biznes."*

"Kto ty!" someone yells behind me. Swinging around, a gun points at me, their finger too close to the trigger for comfort.

"Uh, what?" My hands twist together, my heart pounding as the memories come racing forward. The number of times they pulled a gun on me, the number of times I've been pistol whipped.

"Spuskat'sya. Idi k chertu!"

Shaking my head, I don't understand what he's saying. Why is he yelling at me?

"I..I." My voice shakes…*Jesse stands there in front of me, his gun pressed against my head. The threats of blowing my brains out. I know he means it; I know he does. No one but Izel cares about me here. No one cares about us. We're used as punching bags, we're nothing.*

"POLUCHAYTE NAKHER. SEYCHAS!" I'm brought back, the cool touch of metal presses against my forehead. My eyes slowly adjusted to the fact I hadn't noticed him moving forward, or the fact he was still screaming words at me. I couldn't understand what he was saying. It was all a different language.

I step back, trying to put some space between us, but as I try to come up with my escape plan, he lunges for me. My body twists around, my back up against his chest, bile rising in my throat.

"Let me go," I whimper, my voice failing, the anger coursing through my veins. But as much anger as I feel, fear crawls its way through my skin. I'm trapped. There is no way I can fight this guy. I'm short for a male, I'm skinny, and weaker than a damn rat against a fucking trap.

"Ostanovis." That familiar voice calls from behind us. Both of our bodies freeze, only I relax because I know that voice. I might not fully know him, but I have the odd sensation that he won't hurt me.

"YA nashel yego kopayushchimsya v tvoikh veshchakh," the man holding onto me growls, refusing to back down. I don't know why he's not listening, but the suit man suddenly rips him away, causing my body to fall against the desk.

"Kogda ya tebe prikazyvayu, ty, chert voz'mi, slushayesh'. Vy ponimayete?" he growls. Turning my head around, my eyes drop down to his hands fisted at his side.

"Da," the other grunts, anger filling the air.

"Podozhdi na postu," suit man orders, his shoulders shaking as he breathes heavily. I don't see the man leaving, just the sound of the door quietly being shut. Now a normal, sane person would probably start freaking out, maybe even run for the hills. But I've never been normal, probably from the number of times I was dropped on the head.

"It's not polite to cum on someone's face and not at least get them off." *What the fuck? Why did I just say that?* Out of everything I could have said, literally anything in the world, I chose to tell him that.

"Hmmm," he hums, shoving those hands into his pockets. My eyes drop to his ass. I never got the chance to look at it before. But now, *damn,* I might not be a top, but that doesn't mean I don't want to devour that peach.

"It's not." I might as well go with it. "Also, do you ever plan on telling me your name?" I ask, fidgeting. I don't like staring at his back, and I don't like that he's once again refusing to say anything to me.

When he doesn't say anything, I decide to pull my inner sister out and walk around his desk. Sitting down, I kick my legs up and decide to get comfortable. He obviously works here, which means the only way he'll get me to move is if he talks to me. Ha, one for Gabriel, zero for suit man.

Slowly he turns around, raising a brow when he sees me not in fact standing behind him, but instead sitting at his desk.

 "Silence bothers me. I don't do well with it either. Which you know it's kind of weird with the way I grew up. So, let's talk, or well since you don't seem in the mood to talk, just nod your head. Will that work for you? You know, my sister's husband was the same way when they first met. He looked at her like she was crazy because she talks nonstop. Even to this day." I laugh, remembering when I first met him. His gun was aimed at me, and Izel just walked up to him, waving her hand, ordering him to put it away. Then I drowned myself in Mcdonalds', and the rest was history.

And just like how Zion used to stare at Izel, like she needed to stop talking was the same way this man was staring at me. For some reason, I didn't mind. I liked that he was confused.

"So, first question I got, did you..." Using my finger, I slid it across my neck. "Yah know, Billy?"

Slowly, turtle slow, he nodded his head.

"Interesting. Well, thank you for that. You know, the question you had asked earlier, about him hitting me? He hit me once before, a few days before that night. He was asking about you, wanting to know if I said anything about him."

Suit man crossed his arms over his chest, narrowing his eyes at me. I'd like to think he was getting mad because someone hurt me and not being that I did something.

Suddenly it dawned on me, that he might think I *did* tell Billy something, even if I don't know anything.

"Shit." Sitting up, my feet hit the ground, my hand smacking against the desk. "I promise I didn't say anything! I mean I don't even know anything, honestly. I don't know who you are. I mean the first time I even met you, you broke in. And continue to break in, not that I even called the police."

I need to stop talking.

"Because I didn't. I mean, even if I had, I'm not sure what I would even tell them. It's not like I can just say some attractive man broke in and keeps doing so, yah know leaving stuff behind..."

Jesus, Gabriel, shut up.

"And lord, did you take me by surprise. I mean, I couldn't stop looking at your hands." Stop. Talking. "Especially when you wrapped that hand around my throat."

Oh, fuck me. I can't stop talking, nor could I stop the groan that slipped through my mouth. He doesn't need to know I dream, or hell even think about him. Even if he sneaks into the room when I sleep and jerks off on my face.

"Wow, look at me. Unable to stop talking. I said I was going to ask questions and all I've done is talk and talk."

"Tobias," he whispers.

My head snaps up, unbelieving that he even spoke and that he's telling me his name.

"Tobias," I repeat, testing his name on my lips, loving the idea that now I have a name to pleasure myself with.

His eyes widen, the slight tick in his jaw. I expect him to be mad or upset. But the way he's staring at me, it's more predatory.

"Can you tell me why you were stalking me?" I ask, needing to get away from any ideas that are swarming around in my head. Tobias rolls his eyes, dropping into the chair across from the desk. We stare at each other for a long minute, getting lost in those green eyes. My fingers itch for something to draw with, the angle of his eyes.

"I wasn't stalking you," he finally answers, crossing his leg over the other.

Smiling up, I can't help but laugh. "That's exactly what you were doing. I mean, are you going to tell me it wasn't you that broke into my apartment for over a month, leaving behind paintbrushes for me to find?"

Tobias scoffs, rolling his eyes before glancing away. A hint of pink lightens his face, and that's how I truly know it was him. He wouldn't be blushing if it weren't him.

"Exactly!" I point my finger at him. "That little blush tells me everything."

"I'm not blushing," he growls, narrowing those gorgeous eyes at me.

"Oh, is that right? Are you going to say it's hot in here?"

"It is."

Tilting my head to the side, I study him once more. The first time we met, I was nervous and a little scared. Sure, I was turned on. But I was also nervous he was going to murder me if I said or did anything.

But that feeling wasn't there anymore. Probably because I knew it was him all along, or because he just saved me from whoever that guy was.

"Why are you staring at me?" Tobias asks, breaking into my thoughts.

Shrugging my shoulders, I sit back against the chair.

"I don't like repeating myself."

"You've said that to me before." Remembering when I was too distracted by his hands, and the smell of smoke that clung to his skin.

"And I'm telling you again."

"What are you telling me?" I ask, smirking. Because I know exactly what he's asking, but the idea of him getting out of the chair, grabbing me by the throat again... Or he could just shove them up my as–

"Pakhan." The door slams open, and another man stands at the doorway.

"Da," Tobias answers, not breaking eye contact from me.

"Boris tam boltayet o nem."

I really need to learn Russian or get my hands on some type of translation. I don't like not knowing what they're saying, not being clued in; it feels like they're talking about me. And when the man in the doorway glances over at me, I know the truth. Whatever is being said is definitely about me.

"Kto tam voobshche?" Tobias asks, still refusing to look away from me.

I shift, feeling uncomfortable that both of them are watching. I mean, I have no idea what they're even saying.

"Boris, Lev, Oleg, and Pavel."

It doesn't take a genius to know those are names, but the nagging question is, what are they talking about? And don't they know it's rude to talk in another language in front of those who can't eavesdrop?

"Boris prichinil bol' Gabriel, ya sobirayus' prepodat' yemu urok."
My name was clear and now even if I had a little doubt, they were
talking about me, it was clear now.

"It's rude to talk about someone when they're right here," I hiss,
rolling my eyes.

Tobias smiles, tilting his head to the side.

"My apologies, Little Rabbit." Getting to his feet, he adjusts his suit
jacket. "I have some business to attend to. You can wander all you like,
just not outside, not until I can show you around." Walking around
the desk, he steps close enough I can feel the heat from his body. My
eyes travel up, and my breath catches when he slowly bends down,
each arm sitting on the armrest. "And I mean it, no outside...and I
wouldn't go downstairs. You won't like the consequences if I find out
you've disobeyed me."

Oh, fuck me. I think I would like those consequences.

Tobias stands, not glancing back once before he's walking out of the
office, the door closed. Leaving me alone with the idea of disobeying
him, and my dick getting hard with the idea.

I really shouldn't disobey him. But then again, I don't listen very
well.

11

Tobias

Teaching him a lesson as in I'm going to murder Boris slowly. I'm going to pull his guts out, slowly, and force everyone to watch as I remove every single organ from that piece of shit. Gabriel is mine, mine to touch, fucking *mine.* It took everything in me not to murder him right there in the office. But I couldn't scare Gabriel. He needed to know who I was before he found out I've murdered people. Sure, he knew Billy, but he doesn't know that it's what I do for a living. He might not even know what Billy did.

"So…" Humor filled Kyler's voice. "Are we going to talk about it?"

Walking through the kitchen, we step outside into the cool air, the wind picking up. Pulling out a cigarette I light it, inhaling the pure bliss.

"He was sitting at your desk," Kyler scoffs. "I'm not even allowed to sit there. The last time I tried you broke my nose."

Smiling against my cigarette, Kyler tried a few years ago when this house was freshly built to sit behind my desk. I walked in to find him getting comfortable, and though I didn't have a good reason, I had banned anyone behind my desk since then. Even Kyler.

"What happened with Boris and Gabriel?" Kyler asks as we follow the stepping-stones down to a small warehouse I have in the back of the property. It's where most of the guards sleep, and where Boris is going to die.

"I, uh, I wasn't stalking, but I saw that Gabriel was snooping around. When he went into my office, Boris followed and put his hands on Gabriel," I growled, taking the last drag of my cigarette.

"You seem, well, extremely protective of this guy."

It's a sign of weakness. We both know this. In the Mafia, showing you outright care for another person, especially your wife or in my case another guy, they become a target, even with my own men behind me. You can't trust anyone; your own can turn on you at any given moment. So, I walked into the guards' sleeping area to order them to leave Gabriel alone and that if I hear or see any of them touching Gabriel, I'll kill them.

I don't say anything. Flicking the butt of my cigarette into the sand cup next to the door, Kyler and I step into the small warehouse. All ten guards that aren't on duty are there, along with Boris who stops laughing the moment I step into the area.

"Attention!" I yell. Watching as each of them line up, hands behind their back waiting for my order. The feeling never gets old, the power, all of it, sitting in the palm of my hand.

Kyler stands behind me, as he always does. While I still focus on the men, Kyler does a better job at watching their every move. It only happened once when one of the guards thought it was a good idea to step out of line and question my orders. He's now somewhere in the ocean.

"Boris come here," I order. His eyes widen. I know he thought he got away with what he did. Because not only did he touch Gabriel but didn't listen when I told him to leave him alone. He thought it was a good idea to question me, and for that alone, he deserves to die. No one questions me.

Ever so slowly Boris steps between everyone and makes his way in front of me, leaving a good few feet gap between us.

"When I give an order what do you do?" I ask in Russian, loud enough for everyone to hear. Visible sweat drips from his forehead, and his tongue darts out as he nervously twitches. Good.

When he doesn't speak, I step closer, my height towering over him. I might not be extremely tall, but at six foot three, it's more than the average, but it's enough on Boris.

"Hold your right hand out," I demand. Too slow for my liking, Boris shakes as he holds his hand out. Kyler steps forward and when I give him the slightest nod, only Kyler knows what I mean. He pulls his hand machete from behind his back, swinging it down onto Boris' right hand. Cutting it clean off, blood sprays everywhere, and he screams at the top of his lungs. Gasps fill the room before it becomes dead silent.

"When I give a fucking order..." Backing away from Boris, I face my men. "I expect you ALL TO FUCKING OBEY!" I yell. I was angry before, but now I'm furious. It takes everything in me to not truly kill Boris. But now with one less hand, maybe he'll get himself killed. The enemy can take care of the dirty work for me.

"Da, Pakhan," everyone yells, some of them frowning at Boris, who's barely awake with the amount of blood dripping onto the floor.

"Gabriel is off limits," I say, hoping this doesn't come back to bite me in the ass. I need to make a trip back to Russia and tell my father that I apparently don't seem to be all that straight. But the thought of even leaving Gabriel, makes my skin crawl, my insides burn. I'll probably just have to force him to come with me. One way or the other. I don't think it would be that hard. Finally sitting down and talking to him, it's not all that bad. Though he did most of the talking, that chatterbox.

"If I see you talking to him, I'll cut your tongue off. If I see you touching him, I will chop your hand off. None of you will speak to him or touch him. Do I make myself clear?"

"Da, Pakhan."

"Disrespect him and you're disrespecting me. Do it, and I will kill you."

"Da, Pakhan."

"Boris is just an example of what I will do if you touch him," I state, turning back towards Boris, as he stands holding his hand against his chest. The fucker is probably going to bleed out from the looks of it.

"Boris, kneel."

Getting to his knees, I step over in front of him. "Stick your tongue out."

Boris shakes his head, tears rolling down his cheek. Holding my hand out, Kyler places a knife into my waiting hand before stepping behind Boris. Nodding once more, Kyler grips Boris' head, holding him tight. I hear movement in the door, but I don't look. I expect it's

Gabriel, not being able to follow my simple order. Good, let him watch the monster I am.

Prying his jaw open, I rip his tongue from his mouth, taking the knife I cut through his tongue. Blood soaks his chin, pouring to the ground. My hands are soaked, and when I hold his tongue up, I hear a faint whisper, "Oh fuck." My head snaps to the door, where Gabriel is sure enough watching. Gone pale white, he swallows but doesn't back away.

"Let this be a lesson," I growl, switching to English. I shove his tongue back into his mouth. Kyler steps back, narrowing his eyes at the men. Boris falls to his side, his body going limp. "Fail to listen to my orders and this will be you."

Guess no one is going to have to kill him since I just did.

Turning my back to everyone, I walk towards Gabriel who slowly backs out but doesn't run. Interesting. The moment I slam the door closed, Gabriel looks towards the house, probably debating if he could make it there before I caught him.

"Are you going to hurt me?" he asks, twisting his fingers together. Something I've noticed he does when he's nervous or unsure of himself.

"Do you want me to hurt you?" I ask, pulling out another cigarette.

"I, well, I don't really do well with pain." His eyes drop to my cigarette and bloody arm. I'm not sure I like that answer, but I won't comment. I don't want to spook the poor man, even if I did just cut a man's tongue out for him.

"Are you some sort of hitman?"

Tilting my head to the side, I wonder what he knows about them. I've met a few, the most popular, Devil, but he was killed over fifteen years ago by Killian. Devil turned out to have been a long-lost friend of Killian and Aziza but held a grudge against Aziza for some reason. He ended up kidnapping and torturing her for a day before some girl broke her out and Killian left to kill him. I don't know or remember too much of that time because I was seven and my parents decided to go back to Russia when Blake was born.

Then there was The Butcher, which no one has heard from or about in years. Two rumors circle around, that he's either dead or retired. Either way, from the stories, The Butcher is not someone you ever want to meet.

Realizing I'm still staring at him, I shake my head, motioning for us to start walking towards the house. Gabriel sighs and starts walking ahead.

"Please tell me you didn't just kill him because of me," Gabriel finally speaks, filling the silence.

I debate telling him that it is all his fault. But that isn't entirely true. "No, Boris, the guy, he has an issue with orders, and while that's fine in some areas, it's not okay when I'm his boss, and he knows what he can and can't do."

"Hmmm, boss? So, what do you do then, to be a boss?"

"Well, I was born into it. I didn't have much of a choice." Rushing, I open the back door leading into the kitchen. When was the last time I opened a door for someone else?

"Thank you." Gabriel smiles, his cheeks turning a tint of pink. I shouldn't feel my sides turning at knowing I made him blush. But fuck, it feels good.

"You hungry?" I ask. I'd do just about anything to keep him here talking, just to be around him.

"I could eat. It's been a few hours." Gabriel chuckles, eyes darting around the kitchen. "But I have to warn you, I'm not a good cook. I don't imagine you're a cook, not to be rude. You just don't look like a type that would cook. My sister's husband cooks a lot." Gabriel's cheeks turn a bright shade of red, realizing he's giving me more information than he'd probably like.

"Well, for your information, I love to cook," I smirk. "Just let me go clean up and I'll be back."

Gabriel nods, and I run off. I probably take the world's fastest shower, nearly slipping on the tile floor in my bathroom. And when I pick my clothes out, I spend too long trying to figure out what dress shirt Gabriel would like. Finally picking out a black one and black dress pants I race back downstairs, hoping he hasn't decided to run off.

The moment I see Gabriel sitting there, his legs moving back and forth, I chuckle at how cute he looks.

"Fuck," he curses, grabbing at his chest. "You scared me. You know it's not very polite to sneak up on someone."

"Moi izvineniya," I mutter, walking around him. I begin pulling out all the dry ingredients, before grabbing eggs from the fridge.

"What does that mean?"

Pulling a bowl down, I heat a pan up before I begin pouring the ingredients together. It isn't my intention to ignore Gabriel, but I know if I don't focus on the task at hand, I'm going to fumble through making him food. And that would not be a good look.

"Helloooo?" Gabriel huffs from behind me.

"Do you like Blinchiki?" I ask instead.

"What's Blich-Bleich... whatever you just called this," Gabriel asks, waving a hand at the mixing bowl. Chuckling, I glance up, shocked to see him actually leaning over the kitchen island watching me intently.

"Blinchiki," I pronounce again for him. "It basically translates to pancakes in English. But it tastes and kind of looks like crepes."

"Oh, fancy. I like crepes, especially when you put a little Nutella on top. And if you add fruit. Oh man, tell me you have some, you have fruit, right?"

"Uh, I believe, yeah. You can look in the fridge," I mumble, realizing this feels and sounds very domestic to me.

Gabriel jumps from the chair, racing over to the fridge. Ripping the door open he shuffles through before I hear it close. Pouring some batter onto the hot pan, I feel Gabriel opening and closing cabinets.

"Find what you're looking for?" I ask, finding it a little comical that he gives no fucks about going through my house. Even if I should be scared or nervous that he might find something he's not supposed to. I can't hide the fact I like it. I enjoy him being here. It's where I can keep a close eye on him, closer than breaking into his apartment and watching him sleep.

"Just snooping," he mutters, opening another cabinet. "Ah-ha!" He chuckles.

Finishing up the one blinchiki, I set it aside before peeking over at what he found. What I didn't expect was to find Gabriel shoving a donut I didn't know we had here into his mouth.

"What?" Gabriel smiles around a mouthful of food.

Fuck, he is so damn fine. The shaggy blond hair that curls around his ears, the cute dimple in his left cheek whenever he smiles big... I want to see his dusky nipples again, the curve of his ass. My cock begins to swell before I can help it.

"I think your crepes are burning..." Gabriel says, pointing to the pan. Whipping my head back, sure enough the one in the pan is burning and all I can think about is shoving my cock into his mouth before forcing him on his stomach and pounding into his ass.

"Tobias?" Gabriel steps closer to me, shoving the rest of the donut into his mouth.

"I, uh... I just remembered I have some business to take care of. Go ahead and eat," I blurt out. Shoving my way between him and the island I run to the hallway, bypassing his room and rushing to mine.

I am being a coward, and my father would be ashamed if he saw me like this. But fuck, Gabriel is messing with my head, and no matter if I want him or not, this is not going to end well for either of us.

12

Gabriel

I thought me and my stalker were finally coming to an understanding. Granted, we've talked twice, barely. But he let me wander around his house. I snooped through every damn inch. Well, most of it. I haven't dared to look around his office or bedroom. Sure, I opened his door, but the moment I did, I was hit with his smell, smoke lingering, but some cologne filled my nostrils. I wanted so desperately to go through all his belongings, but it felt wrong and a little too personal.

I also haven't stepped foot in his office, the idea of another guard finding me and the flashbacks coming back. No thank you. I'd rather stick my hand into a pot of boiling water.

But I also would love to know why, ever since Tobias ran off after burning those pancake things, he's been avoiding me. It's been lonely, and I don't like it. The first day I snooped through mostly everything. The second day, I tracked Amy down and though she was reluctant to tell me anything, she kept me company for most of the day.

Which makes today the third day. For three whole days Tobias has been ignoring me, and is nowhere to be found. But every night he comes in, watches me for hours, and sometimes I can feel him pushing my hair out of my face. I fight against wanting to lean into his touch but stop because whatever happened with him the other night, something spooked him.

I'm not sure if it's because I was snooping around in front of him. I was honestly looking for something sweet. I've been dying for some donuts, and when I found some, I couldn't stop myself from indulging in them.

That's why here I am, finishing up this burnt meal. Serves him right for ignoring me, I was left to enjoy those pancake things. Whatever that name is that Tobias called them, I ate every single one, even the damn burned one he left behind. I stayed up for hours, waiting for him to come back, but he never did. I shouldn't have been hurt. I don't know the dude.

But he can't keep sneaking into my apartment, let alone take me in the middle of the night, and not explain himself.

So here I am, carrying a plate of half-burnt pancakes and a glass of milk as a peace offering. He needs to either explain what I'm doing here or let me go with no word. I can't be a prisoner.

Shuffling the plate over, I don't knock, knowing that he is probably watching me somehow. He has to have a way of avoiding me, and it's either he's really good at sneaking around or he has a camera system somewhere around here.

But what I don't expect is to find not only him sitting at his desk, but a group of five men all standing in front. My breath hitches when each one of them narrows their eyes and makes a move to stand.

"Stoy, chert voz'mi, vniz," he barks.

Opening my mouth to apologize so I can tuck my tail between my legs and run, I stop when he glares at me.

"Vse vyshli, idite na svoy post." I have no idea what he said again, and I think about throwing this plate of barely edible food at him. But when the men all stand, all nodding their heads at Tobias before heading towards the door, heading towards me, I squeeze myself against the wall, nerves wracking my body. When the last one walks out, closing the door quietly behind himself, I'm at a loss on what to do. I was so confident, and now that I'm here, I'm really questioning my decision.

So, when I say, "You've been avoiding me," I want to throw myself out the window.

Tobias continues to glare at me as I chew on my lip, my nerves getting worse.

Stepping forward, I set the plate of pancakes and glass of milk down. "I brought you food. I kind of burnt them. I mean, I'm not a good cook. I can't cook at all, really. But you made me food and left me to eat it all alone, so here... I made you food and I expect you to eat it." I take a deep breath. "Alone."

When Tobias doesn't say anything, I bite my inner cheek to stop myself from saying anything else. I don't need to word vomit any more than I already have. Turning on my heel, my body trembles and I know I fucked up. I shouldn't have tried to see him.

"Little Rabbit," Tobias calls softly.

"Yes?" Glancing over my shoulder, my hand stays on the doorknob.

"Come here," he orders. I shouldn't, but my feet move on their own. Tobias stands and walks around his desk. Taking a seat, I stand off to the side waiting for what he wants. "Take a seat... at my desk," he adds when I step over the chair next to him.

Doing as he asks, I sit down and refuse to make eye contact with him. It's a long minute, or two. I don't know how long it is that we just sit there. Complete silence. It's driving me insane; my skin is on fire. My heart speeds up, at the reminder that when men get quiet, it means they are mad. Dan always got really quiet before all hell broke loose and he'd beat me.

"I want to go home," I blurt out.

Tobias' head snaps up, scowling at me like I just kicked his puppy. Shaking his head, he bends forward, grabbing the plate. I watch as he cuts into one with the fork, shoving it into his mouth. Now I know I'm a bad cook. I've tried since Zion saved Izel and me. But no one taught me. Zion never had the patience, and honestly, I didn't care if he taught me or not. I lived off microwaveable meals, ramen noodles, and takeout since I left their house. So, when Tobias barely chews and just swallows that bite, I know he hates it.

"I never learned to cook; Dan never taught us. And my sister's husband, he tried once, maybe twice but lost patience when I got off track and ended up burning the toast or giving them rubbery eggs. So usually, I live off things I can put in the microwave, those types of things. But you know, you made me whatever those things were a few days ago. So, I thought I would make pancakes." Again, I can't stop talking, and Tobias just watches me, cutting into another pancake.

"Alright, this has been a fun conversation, I'm going to go–"

"I can teach you to cook," Tobias blurts out. "Let's go."

And like an obedient dog, I follow him out of the office and into the kitchen. Tobias walks around the kitchen, moving the dirty dishes I left out into the sink before pulling out ingredients for pancakes.

"Come here, I won't bite," he smirks.

My cock twitches between my legs, my balls tingle, and the idea of getting on my knees for him pops into my head. *I'm so screwed.*

"We're going to start off with simple pancakes."

"Oh, were the ones I made that bad?"

Tobias inclines his head as if to say, *"Are you serious?"* But they couldn't have been that bad… I don't think so. Measuring out the pancake batter and then adding an egg and some milk, he stirs it. My eyes drop down to his hands, the veins popping out as he uses the spoon. *Oh fuck.* I am totally and completely fucked. His hands would look so good around my neck as he pounded into me.

I really need to get a hold of my dildos.

"Little Rabbit," Tobias says, bringing me back.

"Fuck, sorry," I mumble, realizing this is exactly why Zion hated trying to teach me. I got distracted and ended up forgetting what I was doing. I also often walked away trying to get something else done when I ended up remembering that I was in the middle of cooking.

It's a problem.

"Gabriel."

"Shit, yeah. I'm here." I smile at him.

"Okay, now I'm going to have you put some butter into the pan to heat up."

Doing as he asks, Tobias stands to the side watching my every move. Normally I would get nervous and hated when Zion did this. But with him, it feels almost natural. It feels nice and… too comfortable.

"Okay, now I'm going to have you use this small measuring cup and pour a little into the pan. Do about three pancakes, leaving enough room in between to leave them alone to cook evenly."

Taking a deep breath, I follow his instructions, not wanting to mess this up. My eyes squint in concentration. The warmth of Tobias behind me only makes me fuck up pouring the mix into the pan a few times.

I swear I hear him chuckle, but don't turn around, scared he'll run away like the last time. Adjusting my stance, I purposely bump into him a little, and when he doesn't move my heart speeds up a little more. I'm playing with fire here. I think he's straight, but I hope he might be bisexual.

"Okay, it's time to flip, Little Rabbit," Tobias whispers a little too close to my ear. I shiver, my hand trembling as I flip each pancake, only messing up on all three. "It's okay, they'll still cook and taste good."

I bet he tastes good. The things I would do to him. I wonder if he likes his ass to be played with. I have a great tongue, and I could do wonders with his body.

"Little Rabbit." Tobias once again pulls me back. I've got to get my shit under control. I can't just keep imagining the things I want him to do to my body or what I want to do to him.

"I think they're done," Tobias whispers, picking up the spatula and holding it out to me. Right, I'm supposed to be focusing on not burning these pancakes instead of Tobias railing into me.

"Right," I mutter, picking up the spatula from his hand. Our fingers brush and I swear my cock grows even harder. I pray he doesn't notice, and that when this is all over, he doesn't have cameras in the bathroom. Because I'm going to need an ice-cold shower to calm this thing down.

"When can I have my phone?" I ask. Izel must have texted or called me at some point and if I don't answer I'm sure she will use the stupid tracker in my arm.

"I'm not sure," he mumbles. Letting me go, I flip the pancake.

"Oh," I mutter, unsure of what else there is to say. Thankfully, after the first batch things calm down. Tobias gives me a little more space, and I don't burn the food, nor are they undercooked. Tobias doesn't talk much, letting me babble about everything I can think of. Mostly I speak about my art and how it was a struggle at first to get students. I don't bring up my phone again, realizing he's probably scared I'm going to run, but for some reason, I don't want to. I want to stay here with him, this stranger that feels more than anyone I've ever met before.

He doesn't run away when I finish making the food, and even sits down at the island with me. Though he barely makes a peep while we eat, I still count that as a win. And when he excuses himself after helping me clean up, I'm only slightly disappointed.

13

Tobias

I stand by the window, watching Gabriel as he walks closer and closer to the tree line. My jaw tightens, remembering clearly that I told him not to go outside until I showed him. But of course, there he is, clearly not listening to me. Clearly, he needs to be taught a lesson. Hmm, him bent over my lap, ass up while I spanked his pale ass. Groaning, I press a hand against my growing cock.

Suddenly Gabriel stops moving, his gaze snapping to the left. I follow where he's looking, only I don't see anything.

"What are you looking at, Little Rabbit?" I whisper, squinting my eyes, basically pressing my face against the glass window. Gabriel continues on moving, taking a few steps to the right, when all of a sudden, he stops, and movement catches my eye.

Shit.

Grabbing my gun from the desk, I run out of the office into the backyard.

"Gabriel!" I yell, trying to get his attention, only he doesn't hear me. The fucker who's creeping in my backyard does though and moves towards Gabriel. Fuck, why can't he hear me?

I break out into a run, my dress shoes are definitely not made for this shit. "Goddamn it." I might be fit, but running is not for the weak.

"Gabriel!" I yell a little louder. His head whips towards me, just as the guy is a few feet away from him. He doesn't get a chance to move before he's tackled to the ground, and I hear Gabriel's scream.

I would try and take whoever it is out, but the fear of missing and hitting Gabriel stops me. Pushing my legs faster, I'm there in no time but it only feels like it takes forever. Grabbing the back of the mystery dude's neck, I pull him off Gabriel.

Spinning around, I barely flinch when the knife he's holding slices through my side. I'm filled with so much adrenaline that I'm hitting the guy over and over again, not caring he's stabbed me twice.

"Who are you?" I growl, barely holding onto my anger.

"Fuck you." He spits at me. Blood falls from his mouth, some of it landing on my cheek.

"I won't ask again." Shoving him, he grunts when his back hits the ground.

"I'm not telling you shit," he hisses, waving the knife once more at me. Quick and easy I shoot his hand, blood flying, most of it over my white dress shirt.

"Him or me?" It's all I really need to know. Either way, I'm going to protect him. I'll kill anyone who threatens to hurt Gabriel. He's mine, and only mine to hurt.

He smirks up at me as if he won something. It only fuels my anger. The better part of my brain knows I should drag his sorry ass back to the house, and tie him up in the basement. But I don't.

Aiming, I give him a clean shot in the head. And then a few more in the chest, for good measure.

"Damn," Gabriel says behind me.

How could I have forgotten he was here, that he was going to witness me murdering someone?

Fuck.

I turn towards Gabriel, ready to plead my case. To tell him anything that will make him not run for the hills when my vision blurs. My knees buckle and I go down. Way to be such a fucking pussy.

Gabriel

Take a nice walk outside. It will be fun.

Well, fuck that guard, whoever it was. This was not a good walk, and it was surely not fun. Especially when Tobias falls down like a sack of shit.

"Fuck," I mumble. Tobias takes a shaky breath, his hand going to his side when my eyes seem to finally catch up to realize his white dress is covered in blood.

His blood.

"Fuck!" Dropping to my knees, "Fuck, fuck, fuck," I mutter, my heart racing as I reach forward pressing my bare hand to his shirt. Blood coats my hand. "There's too much," I whisper.

"You say fuck too much." Tobias tries to chuckle only grunts in pain.

"Stop it," I hiss, pulling my shirt over my head, and press it to his side. "There's a lot of blood, baby. Fuck."

"Little Rabbit, breathe. I've been through worse." Again, he tries to laugh.

"Stop it. I told you to stop. This isn't a laughing matter. You're literally bleeding out," I hiss, pressing the shirt harder against him. Tobias grunts, glaring at me. "I told you to stop," I hiss, reaching into my pocket for where my phone normally is, but of course I have yet to receive the thing.

"Fuck, fuck, fuck!" I growl. Why won't he give me my phone? "Well, this is perfect. You're going to bleed out and I'm going to be stranded here. I don't like being left alone." Looking around, I feel the panic racing through my veins. This isn't the time to panic, but fuck. I don't do well on my own. Sure, I live by myself, but suddenly thinking about being on my own without Tobias, the nerves are going to get the best of me when I need to be strong for him.

"You're so beautiful," Tobias says, breaking into my thoughts.

"What?" Glancing down, I take notice that he's smiling and no hint of hurting in sight.

"You're beautiful. And even more so when you're worried."

"What are you talking about?" Was I dreaming? He is surely not making any sense.

"Little Rabbit…" I don't like the way he's saying that. I don't like it at all. "This isn't all my blood." Carefully taking my hand in his, he pulls our hands away from his wound. Lifting and untucking his blood-soaked shirt up, I stare in shock. He pulls it up enough that I gawk at his rock-hard abs. Really nice abs if I may say. Like *really nice.*

"Gabby?" Tobias whispers.

"Hmm?" I hum, my eyes traveling down to the two small stab wounds. Though they don't appear to have done much damage.

"Soooo, you're telling me… I, uh, freaked out for nothing?" Dropping my hand from his, I sit back, my fingers immediately twisting together. My eyes glued to the blood spots laying against my palm.

"It happens."

Rolling my eyes, I snatch my shirt up and get to my feet. I'm not sure if I'm more embarrassed that I just had a teeny, tiny, very small, *microscopic* freak-out. Or if I'm upset that he didn't stop me right away. He let me just believe he was hurt.

"Fuck you." I decide I'm madder at him. Turning towards the house. I take a much-needed breath. Flashbacks of Izel coming into my room barely holding herself together. Bleeding everywhere. My heart hurts, everything hurts, remembering what Dan put us through.

"Don't be mad."

"I'm not."

"Yes, you are," Tobias grunts, the sound of him moving around behind me. "Please don't be mad, Gabriel." He sighs, stepping into my view.

"I'm not mad." I'm not. I'm confused about what I'm feeling towards the man who kidnapped me. But also, for the fact that I'm not running for the hills. I was kidnapped and held against my will before.

Barely survived it. And now I'm willing to let Tobias do whatever he wants. I want to be his. But this is all too fast.

Brushing my hair behind my ear, out of my face he frowns. "I don't like seeing you hurt," he mumbles. *Well, me too, buddy*. I don't like being hurt either. But I don't say anything because what is there to say?

"What are you scared of?" Tobias steps closer, barely leaving any room between our bodies. I can feel the heat radiating off his body. "What scares you more, Little Rabbit, the fact I'm still here or the fact that you're starting to fall for me?"

Dragging in a breath, I slam my eyes closed. He's right, I am falling for him. But I don't enjoy the fact he knows or that he's pointing it out.

"Gabriel..." he says, bringing my attention back to him. "What's got you thinking so hard over there?"

Opening my eyes, I finally look at him. His smile takes me back. What the hell am I even doing? What am I doing here? All the questions swarm around my head, demanding to be heard and answered. I have no idea who Tobias is, and yet here I am playing house with my stalker and kidnapper.

So, I say the only thing I can think of is, "You need to let me go."

Stepping away from Tobias' grasp, I don't blink. If I do, I'll cry. Heading towards the house, I don't stop for Amy who's looking at me with concern, I don't even look at the man with black hair, who's even looking a little worried himself. The moment my door comes into view, I practically run for it, slamming and locking it behind me. I'm sure he has a key for it, but at least he'll hopefully take the hint and leave me alone.

With my hands being covered in blood, I know I need a shower. But the moment the water hits my skin, everything breaks free. The tears stream down my face, and my body crumbles to the ground.

Why did I have to fall for the most unavailable man in the world?

"I'm going to murder your sister." Reaper chuckles. I know he's telling the truth, even as a nine-year-old. I may be young, but growing up with Dan and his stupid men, you learn things. You see things. It's not just women being fucked late in the evening. Its women being raped, and forced to take drugs so they don't remember who or what happened.

"I hate you," I grit out. I hate them all. I hate this fucking place. Everything about it.

"Oh, don't worry your pretty little mind about that. She loves what we do to her." Reaper's smile turns sour when I chuck the empty bottle of liquor from the bar at his face. I know it's a mistake the moment I pick the bottled up, but that doesn't stop me from throwing it. Nor does it stop me from picking up another one and chucking.

"Oh, you've done it now, boy." He laughs, getting to his feet. I know what's about to come, yet my feet are planted, ready to fight a grown-ass man. What can a nine-year-old even do against someone four times his size?

Nothing. They can't do anything.

Because the moment he rips his belt from his pants, I scream at the top of my lungs. My feet are finally getting the hint I need to run and run right now. I don't get two feet, before the first hit to my back, my skin burning as my knees give out. I face plant onto the cold sticky ground, his boots pressing against my hand, as his belt comes down once more on my back, the shirt ripping open.

"STOP!" I scream. "STOP!"

"You'd think you and your whore sister would learn that it's not a good idea to mess with us!" he growls, the belt hitting my back. I can feel my blood dripping down my back, and the burning becomes numb. Everything is fading and there's nothing I can do but accept my fate.

I'm going to die.

Tobias

"Find them. I want to know who Billy was involved with. I want to know what this has to do with Rafael, I want to know!" I yell at Kyler, Derek, and Ronan.

Ronan and Derek bow their heads leaving Kyler standing there watching me fume.

"Is the kid alright?" he asks.

"You know I took his license and found out he's thirty." I don't know why I tell him that, but hearing him call Gabriel a kid, it's weird.

"Is he okay?"

Looking up, I stare at my friend. I expect him to be laughing or smirking, but he's not. He actually looks like he cares and wants to know about his well-being.

"He asked me to let him go," I mutter, hating the words coming from my mouth.

"Are you going to?"

I pace around my office. *"You need to let me go."* His words repeat in my head, over again. I can't get those words out. I don't understand why he would say that, or why he would think I would be *willing* to just let him go.

I'm not. He's mine, and he's staying, even if that means locking him away in this house. Tying him to the fucking bed, or in the basement. He's mine, and Gabriel isn't going anywhere. He's fucking mine.

"No." I sigh, hating that I should let him go. But I can't.

I'll just have to work harder at getting him to understand that. I'm not going anywhere, even if he somehow manages to slip from my fingers. I'll follow him again, track him, no matter where he goes. No one else can have him. He's mine.

A scream stops me in my tracks. Who would be screaming like th–

Gabriel.

Kyler and I look at each other before I rip the door open and run towards his room. I burst into his room, Kyler hot on my heels, expecting to find someone hurting him or nearly anything else but him thrashing around on the bed.

"Stop!" he shouts, kicking his legs out.

"I'll let you handle this," Kyler says, closing the door behind him.

Stepping towards him, I dodge his legs, bending to shake his shoulder. The second my hand touches his skin, I get a solid punch to the face.

"Fuck," I grunt.

Tears stream down Gabriel's face, sobbing, limbs thrashing around. My gut clutches at the sight of him being stuck in his nightmare. I've never seen them this bad, especially on him.

"Come on, Gabriel," I coo, climbing into his bed. Wrapping my arms around his shoulders, I try to hold him. Gabriel continues to cry but stops trying to fight against my hold. "Gabriel," I whisper, desperation clawing at my insides, needing him to wake up. This isn't the sassy blond boy I know. The one who refuses to take my shit. I need my boy back. I need my Little Rabbit.

"It's okay, I've got you, I got you," I whisper into his ear.

His body slowly stops struggling, his cry becoming quiet. The only sound is his breathing, a little strained but still there.

"Tobias?" he whispers, his hand reaching back, the soft touch of his fingers against my cheek.

"Yes, Little Rabbit, it's me. I've got you." I sigh into the back of his head.

Gabriel nods his head, taking his hand from my cheek. I almost beg him to put it back, the words dying in my throat when his hand latches onto my hand, the ones that are wrapped around his chest. Holding his back against my chest.

Several long minutes pass. Gabriel's breathing returns slightly normal, and my hold on him tightens. Refusing to let go, even if he wanted me to. I don't know who is holding onto who more. But I am clinging for dear life because he might as well have been.

14

Gabriel

"**W**hat helps you?" Tobias asks, his arm still wrapped around my chest.

I hate how small I feel, how I escaped from Dan, but I'm still stuck in my nightmares. I'm still stuck. But I can't tell him any of that, no. I can't tell anyone that I am still afraid I'm going to be sold, raped, and beaten again. Even though they are dead. It's been fifteen damn years, and I'm still back in that office, waiting for them to take me.

"Gabriel, I can only help if you let me. And I can see that fight, most probably don't see it. But I do. Now tell me. What helps?"

"Drawing, coloring, that sort of thing." I shrug, his arms dropping from my body. Crawling to the edge of my bed.

I know it sounds childish. I mean, when everything went down with my sister and Zion, her husband now, I gravitated toward art. Drawing helped me most of the time. It was my outlet.

"I have an idea." Tobias suddenly stands, ripping his shirt off.

Drool pools in my mouth the moment my eyes land on his hard muscles and they lock on his waist. Especially where a small patch of black coarse hair disappears below his pants.

"I've been thinking of getting something tattooed. My whole family has them. I think it's about time I get something done," he says, his hand disappearing into his dress pants pocket. I have no idea what he's searching for. But suddenly the words he spoke finally catch up and he can't be serious.

"You're joking." I laugh because seriously Tobias can't be... I just...*no.*

"I'm not. I mean you should see my uncle, he has a shit ton. I don't think there's any space left on his skin. Literally. Plus, this way... never mind. I just think a tattoo would be nice." Smirking at me, he pulls out a pen, holding it out for me.

"So, what's your plan then?" I ask, reaching slowly for the stupid pen.

"Draw something on me. Anything, I don't care." Tobias scoots down lying down on my bed.

"Tobias." I sigh, my eyes dropping to the pen sitting in my hand.

"Gabriel."

"I'm not sure. I'm decent, I can somewhat make a living out of it... but drawing on someone's skin. What if, I dunno, it never comes off?"

"It won't. I planned on getting it tattooed eventually. Maybe to-morrow morning, but the pen works for now." Throwing his arms behind his head, he raises a brow at me. Waiting for yet another excuse.

I just don't have one.

Maybe one.

He's looking delicious and all I want to do is rip his pants off to see his package. But he's straight and that would be entirely awkward.

"Okay..." I whisper. Turning over I sit beside him and shakily start on his chest. I'm not even sure what I'm drawing, but I never am.

I let my mind wander, let my feelings go, and just draw. It's how I coped with the past and how I cope with my nightmares now.

I don't know how long it's been since I began drawing on his chest, but when Tobias mumbles, "Kiss me," I sit back, panic rushing through my veins.

"I, uh, I'd rather not." I laugh, refusing to acknowledge the hurt in his eyes. "I've fallen for straight men before and it never ends well. I'd rather not kiss you once and then wonder what it feels like to kiss you whenever I want," I word vomit. I can't look at him anymore, I don't want to see him laugh or smirk knowing he's got the gay kid to fall for him.

"Why can't you kiss me whenever you want?" he asks, his voice small.

"Because I'm gay, duh," I scoff.

"Yeah, so?"

"Dude, are you really that dense? Come on, I mean I'm gay and you're straight. That's literally a recipe—"

"Who said I was straight?" Tobias asks angrily. Whipping my head towards him, sure enough, Tobias is fuming. Brows furrowed, hands fisted at his side as if I kicked his damn dog.

"I mean... aren't you? I mean... I tried not to read too much into the flirting, some guys are just natural flirts, even with guys...." I'm probably not making any sense. I barely understand this myself. I mean, what do I know? I grew up half my life hiding who I was because my nonbiological father hated gays and women and honestly anything that wasn't hookers and drugs.

"I'm not straight," Tobias finally says, still frowning at me.

"So, you're gay?" I ask, a little hope slipping out. I shouldn't get my hopes up, I really shouldn't. But it's there and I can't control it.

"No."

"That doesn't make any sense, love..." I sigh, the fight in me leaving.

Suddenly Tobias is grabbing my face, inching away. "Call me that again."

"Uh, love..."

"Fuck," he growls right before he slams his lips against mine. At first, I'm not sure what to do. I'm motionless, confused about what he's doing. I chalked up the constant staring, the stalking, even the damn flirting to be nothing. And now his lips are on mine.

And he claims to not be gay.

Or straight.

But his lips are soft, warm, and *perfect*. And it's not until he whimpers, fucking *whimpers* against my mouth, that I realize I haven't moved yet.

My hands reach up, cupping his head, tugging his black hair a little. My entire body ignites when he presses closer to me, wrapping an arm around my waist as if he can't get me close enough. I open my mouth and Tobias wastes no time moving his tongue along mine. My toes curl the moment he fully takes over the kiss. I thank the heavens above when he drops his hands down to my ass and squeezes. Grunting when he bites down on my bottom lip hard enough it splits open, only instead of being turned off from the taste of my blood, Tobias moans, sucking my lips into his mouth.

I'm barely aware of him moving me back until my back literally drops onto the bed, and Tobias lies over me. Never breaking the kiss, his hands grip my hair, and *holy fuck shit*. Grinding his crotch against my own, my cock that has already hardened and perked up from the kiss is now solid stone. Demanding attention. My arms wrap around his shoulder, gripping onto him like he's going to disappear.

I know the reality that once this is over, he's going to realize he's not gay. That kissing a boy isn't the same as kissing a girl. He's going to realize that I'm not what he wants, but I can't seem to care. Not when Tobias' hand is suddenly popping the button on my jeans and lowering the fly.

"Tobias," I say, ripping my mouth from his. He taps my hip, and unable to deny him, I lift. Tobias rips my pants and underwear down to my ankles. "I, Tobias?" I furrow my brows. Tobias doesn't say anything. He's frozen as he stares at my cock laying against my stomach. I open my mouth to once again try and get his attention when he buries his face into my crotch, breathing me in.

I gasp, feeling weird that he just literally smelled my dick. He looks up, eyes finding mine when he places a gentle kiss against my crown.

"Fuck." I drop my head, thrusting my hips up. I can't help it, everything he's doing feels so good. I don't even know if I believe that this is his first time. Not when he kisses my crown once more and then sucks me down. Not missing a beat, he hollows his cheeks and *sucks*.

The thoughts of making him stop, to make sure this is what he wants, are lost the moment he shoves my clothes off my ankle and his hands are gripping and grabbing my balls. I'm barely aware I'm thrusting into his mouth until he gags and pulls off.

"Tobias, maybe we sho—AH." Sucking my balls into his mouth, my eyes lock onto his. His mouth full, hand flicks my precum as he slowly jacks me off. He bites down slightly against my balls. A tinge of pain shoots through my body, but I don't care. The way he's staring at me, his hand moving faster and faster, I know I'm about to come. World record, fastest blowjob.

"Come," he says, popping off before sucking my crown. He doesn't move his mouth, sucking my tip as his hand works faster on my length. "Gabriel...." He warns, breathing against me. "I said... come right *fucking now,*" he growls, and with the heat in his eyes I can't hold back. Not even if I wanted to. Tobias hollows his cheeks once more, his lips wrapped around my crown, and I yell out. My orgasm takes me over and I'm shooting down his throat, his tongue giving me no mercy when he licks my slit, drinking down my cum.

I don't know how long we stay like this. Tobias stays with his mouth pressed against me, only his hands are on my thighs, rubbing against the scars that lay there. I lose my breath, hoping he doesn't notice them. Most of my partners haven't and those who had only ran away disgusted when I told them why. After the first couple, I stopped telling them and refused to acknowledge the hurt in their eyes when I wouldn't fill them in on the truth.

"Tell me," Tobias demands, breaking me from my thoughts. I shake my head, willing the tears that are already threatening to break through, to just go away.

Sitting back Tobias nods, jumping off the bed. I try to hide the hurt when he doesn't even glance my way before slamming the door shut. The tears break through and I'm screaming into the pillow. Hating myself for letting him kiss me, for letting him blow me. And most of all, feeling something towards the man that isn't available.

15

Tobias

I could still taste him on my tongue and down my throat. I hadn't expected to enjoy kissing another man or sucking their dick. But the noises from Gabriel only encouraged me to go on, and when he started thrusting into my mouth, letting himself go, I only wanted him to come more than I wanted this cigarette I'm currently sucking down. Only instead of making me feel calm, I'm getting nauseous remembering the scars on Gabriel's thigh.

Fuck.

Flicking my half-smoked cigarette, I throw my head back. I know what those scars are, I just don't know who or why. Yanking my phone out, I pull Emilia's contact up.

"Oh, my favorite cousin," she answers on the first ring.

"I need a favor."

"I get no hello, no how are you, nothing?" she hisses. Emilia, not to her fault, is a lot like her mother, Aziza. Sassy, takes no shit from anyone, including my father. Apparently, before Emilia was even born, she stole a few million from one of his offshore accounts and gave it away. All because he was annoying her.

"Hello, Emilia, how are you?" I ask, leaning my head against the side of the house.

"I am doing wonderful, thanks for asking. Blake and I have been trying to convince our parents for a family vacation. Wouldn't that be fun?"

"No."

"Okay, party pooper, I see something else is on your mind. What's this favor you need?" Emilia huffs.

"News on Gabriel Hollow."

What I expect is for Emilia to start a whole speech on what she found. Both her parents are computer geniuses, and as they say, the apple doesn't fall from the tree.

"I don't have anything." Emilia's words shock me; I'm stunned. What does she mean she doesn't have anything? Emilia is one of the best hackers, following in her parents' footsteps. So, what does she mean she can't find anything?

"Emilia..." I start, the words lost. "What... I'm confused."

"What are you confused about? I haven't been able to find anything on your little friend there. Kyler has filled me in a little bit. When are you going to tell your father?"

I shouldn't be surprised he opened his big mouth and blabbed off, telling her my business when he had absolutely no right or reason to. I don't want to share Gabriel. I want to lock him away and keep him away from anyone that will try and hurt him.

"Kyler shouldn't be opening his big mouth about my business," I mutter.

"Oh, you're just mad because I'm clued in on your little secret. Which for your information, I think is totally awesome. I didn't know you were gay."

"I'm not gay."

"Tobias." Emilia sighs, and because life always wants to fuck me, Kyler comes around the corner frowning.

"Emilia, I don't have time for this. Just look a little harder and get back to me." I hang up, pocketing my phone.

Kyler walks closer, hands shoved in his pocket, uncomfortable. Which is odd because he's never uncomfortable. He's usually the one making others feel that way.

"Just spit it out," I snap, itching for another cigarette.

"You might not like what I'm about to say. You're not going to agree with it either. But as your best friend since we were little I'm going to just come out and say it. You're too distracted and you need to let him go."

He's right. I don't like what he has to say. I hate the words he's speaking and even more I hate that he is right. I know I shouldn't have brought Gabriel into this. I know I should let him go. The stalking, the obsession, the kidnapping. I need to let him go.

"Tobias–"

"You're right," I mutter.

Kyler jerks back in shock, his eyes glancing around. "Am I being punked?" Of course, the fucker would think I'm playing a joke on him. I usually don't ever admit when he's right, but this is the one time I can't hold it in. He's right. Gabriel and I don't make sense. Who knows if he'll even be able to handle me being head of the Russian Mafia in America?

"What are you going to do?"

"I'm not sure."

"You know it'll be better for both him and you." Holding a cigarette out towards me, shaking my head I still can't get the image of those burn scars on Gabriel's thigh.

"Says who?" I snap, not bothering to let him answer. I turn on my heel and head back inside. Heading straight to my office, I slam the door.

I don't care to hear what Kyler thinks I should do. He's never liked a girl long enough to want anything from them but to fuck and dip. I've seen how he treats them. He thinks girls are just common whores and once he's done using them, he leaves. Never giving them a chance to even mutter the word bye.

Kyler doesn't get to tell me I need to make Gabriel leave. Who knows? He might be strong enough to handle my lifestyle. Maybe the only problem will be my father.

Which gives me an instant headache. I never once feared my father. I know he would never physically lay a hand on me. Even if he ever tried, Aunt Salem and Aunt Aziza would make him disappear.

I just need to figure out who is stealing these shipments, end them, and then I can go tell my father I'm gay but only for Gabriel. I don't understand what it is about him, but being around him calms something inside me. He brings a certain side of myself that I didn't realize I had and it's nice; it's different but exciting.

The sound of my phone going off breaks into daydreaming of Gabriel. Glancing down, Aziza's name appears on the screen for two seconds before disappearing. I sigh a moment of relief, only it dies just as quick when it reappears.

"Da," I answer.

"Why do you want to know about Gabriel Hollow?"

That shocks me, not only because it means that Emilia or Kyler must have run their mouths off, most likely Emilia when she couldn't find something again, but also because if Aziza knows, then Uncle Killian knows which means my father knows. It's only going to be a matter of time before I get a phone call from him.

"I don't know what you're talking about."

"Don't play stupid with me. Not only did my daughter ask me for help, my god damn daughter, Tobias. She doesn't work for you or your damn father. It's Killian, remember him? He is the one involved in your shit. Not me, and certainly not my daughter!"

"You're right, I'm sorry." Swirling around in my office chair, I lay my head back against the headrest. I shouldn't have involved Emilia in my business. I just didn't want anyone finding out about him before I was ready.

"I don't care if you're sorry or not. Do not involve her again in your shady business, even if she begs you to. Understand me, Tobias?"

"Yes, Aziza." I grit my teeth.

"Second, now that I'm involved, why do you need to know about Gabriel?"

"I'm not sure."

It's not a complete lie. Mostly but not completely.

"Tobias, I know he's there with you and unless you want me to get his sister and brother-in-law involved, I suggest you tell me."

"How do you know he's there?"

"His phone, I can trace it," she says as if I just asked the dumbest question. It might as well have been. Aziza could find anyone, anywhere.

"I don't care about his sister or brother-in-law."

"You should," Aziza mutters.

"Well, I don't," I growl, irritation clawing at my inside. This phone call is pointless, and it's only getting worse.

"Tobias, his brother-in-law is The B–"

"I don't care who they are!" I yell, throwing my phone across the room, watching it smash into tiny little pieces.

I close my eyes, inhaling the stale air that wraps around me, threatening to drown me.

"Do you want him?" Kyler asks.

Refusing to open my eyes, I nod.

"Words, Tobias, because I'll stand behind whatever you want. But you need to figure out if this is just something you want because it's different and you're bored. Or because you have actual feelings for him."

"I can't explain it, Kyler. He's not someone I thought I would want. He was supposed to just be a stranger who knew Billy. But the moment I stepped into his apartment, something spoke to me. I couldn't hurt him. I couldn't do what we've been taught to do," I say, my eyes blinking up, the emotions pouring from me. Though it feels good to finally face reality, to face what I've been so scared to say out loud. It feels nice.

"Then I will stand behind you." Kyler chuckles, leaning forward on his knees.

"That easy, huh?"

"It's not easy, no. You're like a little brother I never wanted, but that I've accepted I've got. So, if you have feelings for Gabriel then I stand behind you. I'll go to war for you so might as well be for someone you love." Kyler meets my gaze, neither one of us breaking. I give him a nod; it's all either of us need. Knowing that we stand behind each other, knowing that he's always in my corner, means more to me than he'll ever know.

"You going to stop running away from him?"

"I don't... I don't run from him," I huff, knowing full well I was a fucking liar.

"Yes, you do. Literally the moment you find yourself getting comfortable you run off. The guards talk, and plus I've seen you, Tobias. You get comfortable, and poof you run off to some business."

"It's not a lie about business," I state because it's true. In the Mafia, there's always something happening, something going wrong.

"Tobias." Kyler frowns.

Rolling my eyes, I don't take his bait. I know he wants me to fight him on it, wants me to confess that's how I feel. It's true, but he doesn't need to know that.

"When you find someone, I'll be there too." I laugh, deflecting the conversation from me and knowing full-on that Kyler never plans to settle down.

"Now we just have to tell your dad."

Oh, fuck.

16

Gabriel

I open my eyes only to slam them shut at the bright sun from the blinds I forgot to close during my crying fest last night. Sitting up, I glance around the room, stretching my arms above my head. Groaning when my back cracks, I debate on falling back under the covers or facing the day and Tobias. It doesn't take me long when my stomach growls, and the sudden urge to piss has me jumping from the bed and rushing into the bathroom.

Relieving myself, I take a quick shower, ignoring my reflection in the mirror knowing damn well I look rough. Between the bruises barely starting to heal and my eyes being puffy from crying. I just need a large gallon of iced coffee and donuts. Then I can deal with Tobias and his fucking mood swings.

He had no right to get upset with me not wanting to confide in him about my past when I don't even know who he is. He keeps all these secrets, and I'm tired of it. He can't expect me to tell him everything and not tell me shit.

Shoving my legs into another pair of sweatpants and one of Tobias' sweatshirts, I walk out of the room and down the hall leading to the kitchen. I'm fuming by the time I enter, only to stop mid-step when I find not only Tobias sitting at the kitchen table but the one with black hair that always seems to be hanging around.

"You must be Gabriel. It's nice to officially meet you," the strange man says, holding up a cup before sipping on it. Swallowing whatever he drank, he smiles creepily at me. I shiver under his gaze before I realize he spoke to me.

"Uh, yeah," I muttered, unsure of what exactly I should do. I was angry walking in, but now I'm not too sure.

"I'm Kyler, his enforcer," he says, nodding his head towards Tobias. Blinking like an idiot, I can't form the words, the questions that are swarming around my head. "Coffee?"

Once again, I nod my head, feeling uneasy. Stepping back, my skin aches, the tension in my back crumbling my knees. I can feel the weight of everything pushing against my shoulder. I don't know why I have this feeling.

"Gabriel," Tobias says beside me. I blink over at him, the uneasy feeling disappearing instantly. "Kyler make it iced," he orders, and grabbing my hips he pulls me forward. I try to pull away, a weak attempt but at least I can say I tried. He pulls me until his knees hit the chair, and we both fall down onto it. Tobias sits on the chair while I perch on his lap like some showgirl.

"Tobias, I can't just... let me up." Only he doesn't, his hands tighten on my hips, dragging my back to his front.

Looking over at Kyler, who's busy making my iced coffee, I feel weird, and it doesn't help that when I shift trying to get comfortable, I can feel Tobias' hard cock pressing against my ass. I gasp, looking over my shoulder.

"We need to talk." He smiles, wrapping his arms around my waist.

"Yeah, we do, we definitely do," I mutter, unable to process the fact that Tobias not only kissed me, but also gave me the most mind-blowing blowjob, ran out, and is now holding me in his lap in front of someone.

I watch Kyler finish making my coffee, feeling uncomfortable that this stranger made me this. But the moment he mutters something in that language I can't understand, I take a sip and groan as the flavor hits my tongue.

"You shouldn't be making sounds like that when you're sitting in my lap," Tobias growls, his arms tightening around my waist.

"I can get o–"

"No," he hisses, pressing his lips against my shoulder.

"Then let's talk," I huff, sipping my coffee. It's better if I didn't have to look at him anyway. I was never good when confronting others. Call it a flaw, or the fact I was abused as a child. To each their own.

"Ask anything..." Tobias reluctantly says after a minute.

"I have so many. I mean, who are you? I don't even know who you are, yet I have these feelings for you. Why am I here? What happened? I have so much going on up here," I mutter, tapping my temple.

"I'm... well, fuck, I didn't want the first question to be a hard one to answer, but, well... I'm Pakhan, the Mafia boss here in America."

"M–Mafia?" I stutter out, jumping from his lap. Turning around, Tobias seems shocked by the reaction, and well, me too. But I'm already here, and he just... Mafia? Fuck, that's, this is not good.

Tobias must suddenly realize I'm moments from bolting because he's up and out of his seat, stalking toward me. Normally, I cower and beg that he leave me alone. I don't want to be hurt. But Tobias doesn't scare me and that also might be the worst mistake yet.

Wrapping a hand around my throat, he stands toe to toe. "You weren't scared of me when I broke in two months ago, you weren't scared when I stalked you for a month, and you weren't scared of me all this time. So don't suddenly run for the hills because I told you I'm some powerful man."

Rolling my eyes, I bite my lip to stop myself from smiling. Because out of all the things in my life, him being the all-powerful boss doesn't actually scare me. It scares me that I'm having feelings and it's too quick.

"So, you admit you were stalking me?" I smirk, waiting for him to tell me the truth.

Tobias' lips twitch, a hint of amusement flickering in his eyes.

"Tell me the truth, love." I smile, leaning further into his hand.

"Yes," he says immediately. "I'll admit it once, only... only this *once,* Little Rabbit."

It wasn't enough for me. I wanted the words. "Say it," I demand.

Tobias' frown turns into a glare, his hand tightening around my throat. "You're the only one who's ever pushed me back like this."

"Tell me, Tobias," I whisper. With his hand around my neck, his body pressed against mine and the sexual tension between us, my cock is harder than I thought possible, and when his leg presses against my groin I can't help the whimper that escapes my lips.

"Gabriel," Tobias growls. "Fine, I stalked you. I watched you sleep; I watched you all the time. You consumed so much of my life for the past two months. I jerked off to the sight of you. I stood above you and watched you sleep peacefully while I could have easily taken you right there and then. Is that what you wanted to hear?"

The moment I nod, Tobias slams his lips against mine. Releasing my throat, he grabs the back of my thighs and lifts. Wrapping my legs around his waist, I'm aware of him moving, but this kiss is different than it was before. This kiss, we pour everything into it. We're messy, teeth clashing together, our tongues trying to dominate.

I let out a soft grunt when I'm slammed against a wall. Ripping my mouth from his, we're both panting, our gazes locked, something spoken between us. It's a long moment. I'm too afraid to look away, afraid this, whatever this is, will break.

"I want you," Tobias mutters.

"I want you too," I rush out, fear overtaking my every thought.

"No... I want... I want to fuck you." His voice strains, and he presses me harder against the wall, his cock pressing against my ass.

"Tobias... I'm, I'm not sure. It's different with a man." I'm not sure what I'm saying, but I also know that he can't be serious, even if I want him to be more serious than anything else.

Stepping back, I unhook my legs, needing some distance between us.

"I want you."

"I don't want you to regret it."

"I won't. I want you, Gabriel. I want to feel you under me. I want to feel you against my skin. I want you like I've never wanted anyone else," he says, reaching towards me.

And like the weak man that I am, knowing in the end when he gets tired of me it's going to hurt, I whisper, "Okay..."

Tobias smiles, stepping towards me again, and reaching forward.

"Just hold on… let me go, uh, prep myself." I shouldn't be shy. Every gay man needs to prep. But telling Tobias I need to stretch my hole is weird.

"I want to do it," Tobias says, grabbing my shoulder to pull me back.

"No straight man wants to prep another man's hole. It's okay, I'll be right back." I laugh, once again moving out of his reach.

"I told you I'm not straight," Tobias growls.

"You're not gay either," I shoot back, smirking before I turn around to head into the bathroom. I don't make it two steps before Tobias has twisted me around, shoving me against the bed and my pants are ripped down to my ankles. "Whoa, Tobias what are ahhh—"

My words are lost as he spreads my ass cheeks apart and his mouth closes around my hole. My head drops to the mattress, a whimper leaving my mouth. I squeeze my eyes shut, his tongue rimming around my hole, making out with that part of me.

This can't be happening. I'm moments from telling him to stop, that I can prep myself when he presses a finger against my hole. Prodding me, he eases the tip of his finger into me.

"Ohhhh, fuck," I moan.

This feels better than I could have imagined, and when he moans into my ass, I nearly come on the spot. Thrusting my ass back into his mouth, he moans even louder, plunging another finger into my hole.

"Please…" I beg. I don't know what I'm begging for, but anything he'll give me I want. "Please, Tobias, please."

"Hmm, what do you want, Little Rabbit?"

"More, give me more," I beg. My cock hardens, keeping a slow pace with two of his fingers, scissoring me open.

I'm a blubbering mess when he finally sits back, pulling his fingers from my ass. Swinging around my hands go to his pants when Tobias gets to his feet. My hands tremble as I unbutton and pull the zipper down. Ripping them down to his knees, my mouth watering, ready to shove his cock into my mouth when–

"Holy shit." I sit back, my hands dropping from his thighs to my knees. My gaze jumps from his package to his eyes then back down. "Tobias..." I mutter, eying his cock. "That's, you're... whew, Tobias, how do I say this?" I clear my throat, unsure how to say it.

"What?" Tobias asks, stepping out of his pants, and throwing his shirt off.

"Tobias, that thing won't fit in my ass. I'm not sure how it'd fit into anyone's ass or well... you know." His cock is baseball bat hung, Coke can girth, and that doesn't count for the Jacobs ladder or Prince Albert piercings he has.

While he laughs, I scramble backwards hitting my back against the bed frame. There's absolutely no way my ass can take his cock, absolutely no way.

"Where are you going?" Tobias narrows his eyes. *Well, fuck me. I've made the Mafia Pakhan mad. That has got to be the stupidest thing I could have done.* And I'm too wrapped up in my own head to realize Tobias has stepped in front of me. It's not until I feel his hands under my armpits and he's lifting.

"Tobias, I'm not sure. I don't think you'll fit," I say before he throws me onto the bed. Now I'm not small by any means. Five foot seven, one hundred and forty pounds, give or take. But the way Tobias picks me up and throws me around, I might let him actually destroy my ass.

Maybe.

Tobias crawls up my body, forcing me to lie on my back, staring up into his hazel eyes. His thumb brushes over my lips. The way he stares at me, I'm blushing harder than I'd like to admit.

"Are you scared of me?" Tobias' questions surprised me. I'm not sure why he's asking, but the sincerity in his eyes, the flicker of vulnerability that he tries so hard to hide shines through.

"No," I answer honestly. I know pain, I know monsters. Tobias might be the second in charge of the Mafia, learning to take over for his father. But that doesn't mean he'll ever hurt me.

"I'd never hurt you," Tobias whispers, bending to press his lips against my neck. I can't hold my moan in, my hands dragging down his chest to his sides pulling him into me. Our cocks brush up against each other, and I whimper.

"I'll take care of you," he mumbles against my skin. Easing back, he grabs my thighs pushing them to my chest. "Hmmm," he hums, dripping spit onto my hole. Using his cock, he spreads his spit around my hole before his fat tip pushes into me.

"Ohmygod, holllly fuckkk," I groan.

Tobias pushes further into me, not stopping until his hips flush against my ass. My breathing has picked up, and I can feel sweat trickling down my forehead. Digging his fingers into my hips, he pulls out, his piercings dragging inside me.

"Shit, shit, shit," I pant. "Your piercings."

Tobias pulls almost all the way out, the tip of his cock barely holding me open. "Shhh, be a good Little Rabbit and let me fuck this ass. Let me make you feel good." He smiles, thrusting all the way back in.

"Fuuuuuck." My voice breaks, panting as Tobias pounds into me. I've barely gotten used to him being inside. Tobias holds my thighs against my chest, fucking me into the mattress and all I can do is hold on.

My eyes roll into the back of my head, my cock pulses, precum leaking onto my stomach. Reaching down, I squeeze my cock, stroking myself, when suddenly he grips my wrist pulling me away.

"Tobias," I whine, needing to touch myself. I need to cum. It's becoming unbearable. "Tobias, please, I need to cum." I'm not ashamed to beg.

"No," he grunts above me. "Your cock is mine," he states, holding my wrist above my head. Good thing I have another hand. Reaching down, I once again go to grab my cock when Tobias is pulling out of me, flipping me around so I'm lying on my stomach. Twisting my arms to my back, he shoves his cock back into me.

"I told you." Bending until his mouth is near my ear, he licks the column of my neck to my ear. "Your cock is mine," he growls and somehow pounds harder into me. I'm unable to do anything. My ass sticks in the air; my hands are held tightly behind my back. I'm becoming a moaning mess, making inhuman noises. "You're being loud." He laughs, thrusting into me.

I try to say sorry, the words are on the tip of my tongue, but when I open my mouth, he shoves three fingers into my mouth.

"You think they can hear you, Little Rabbit?" He laughs. "I wonder if they think I'm defiling the man I kidnapped," he hisses, biting down on my ear lobe. My entire body tingles, and my ass clenches around his cock.

"Do you think you can cum without touching your cock, Little Rabbit? Think you can be my *good boy* and come with my cock deep in your ass?" Tobias groans, letting go of my hands. I sigh in relief, spreading my arms above my head pushing against the headboard.

"Come in me," I beg. I've never let another man come in me, nor have I ever fucked without a condom. And suddenly I'm realizing Tobias didn't put one on and I don't even know if he's negative.

"Fuck, fuck, Gabriel," Tobias growls, thrusting his hips into me once more before I feel his cock swell just as he comes. My non-touched dick explodes into the mattress. I didn't think I could do it; I truly can't believe I came without my hand or his. And I'm seeing stars, my hands fisting the pillows above me.

"Fuck, Gabriel." Tobias sighs, pulling out of me. I'm left feeling empty and something feels off. I'm used to hookups, casually sleeping with men. But this feels different, and when Tobias doesn't say anything, I'm not sure what to do.

"You're awfully quiet," Tobias mumbles into my ear, pressing his body against my back.

I hum, not trusting the words that are on the tip of my tongue.

"Gabriel," he growls, grabbing my shoulder and flipping me around. Grabbing my wrists he holds them over my head, staring down at me.

"I don't like hookups. I did them a lot when I was in my early twenties, and they left me sad and alone. I'm too old, well not old. I'm only thirty, but I can't do random hookups or friends with benefits. Oh shit, oh no, how old are you?" I rush out, wide eyes as I stare at him.

Tobias is silent as I word vomit. I'm uncomfortable and sweaty and feeling a little used. Tobias doesn't say anything, just stares at me. And when he sits back, letting go of my hands, I do nothing but watch as he moves around the room. Picking up our clothes, he throws them into the laundry basket, and heads to the bathroom.

When he comes out, I hold my legs against my chest, feeling small and unimportant. I hate this feeling and I hate knowing that I just need to grab my clothes before I go back to my room.

Tobias crawls into bed, dragging the blankets up to his waist. When I don't move, he snaps his eyes up to mine, furrowing his brows. "Are you just going to sit there?"

"Oh, right. Um, sorry," I mumble, swinging my legs off to the side of the bed. I don't get a chance to move off the bed before Tobias grabs my arm and yanks me towards him.

"Lay down, Little Rabbit," he mumbles.

Lost at what to say, I start to lie down when he forces my head down onto his chest. Tobias drags the covers up, wrapping an arm around me.

"Tobias, are you cuddling me?" I ask, unable to stop myself from snuggling further into his chest.

"I'm not sure, am I?" He chuckles.

"You are. This... is cuddling."

"Oh, I wasn't sure, I haven't done it before." Tobias sighs. "And for your information, I'm twenty-two."

"Twenty-two... that's, okay," I mutter, feeling more tired than I should be since I just woke up. But I can't help myself when my eyes slowly drift shut.

17

Gabriel

"What's going on?" Kiwi asks, stepping into my room. My eyes snap up to his, rushing forward to close the door. Peeking my head outside I glance around, making sure no one is snooping and eavesdropping. It's the last thing Izel and I need. Not seeing anyone, I close the door behind me.

"Gabe, you're making me nervous, what's going on?" Kiwi asks again, his eyes widening when I point to the bag in the corner. "What's that?"

Closing the distance between us, I lean forward, whispering, "We're leaving."

Izel and I never trust anyone in Dan's clubhouse. They all hurt us. Izel usually gets the worst of it. Kiwi only showed up a few months ago, and instead of hanging out with the other club members he stays with me.

"What do you mean you're leaving?" he blurts out, eyeing the door.

"Shhh," I snap, my hand automatically clamping around his mouth. "Kiwi, we're leaving, Izel and I... we're... we have to leave." Tears glisten in my eyes. I don't want to leave my new friend, but I also can't stay here. We're going to die; we can't stay here....

"Gabe, you can't, you can't leave," he says, almost emotionless.

"We can't stay!" I snap. Why can't he understand? Why isn't he helping me? He knows what they do. He knows, and yet right now he's acting like he couldn't care less.

A sharp knock on the door startles me, my breathing coming in ragged and when I look back at the door and then Kiwi, I whisper, "You can't tell them, you can't," pleading with him to keep his mouth shut.

Kiwi nods before walking around me to open the door. Dan stands on the other side, glaring over Kiwi's shoulder at me. "Office, now," he snaps. Not waiting for Kiwi to answer, he walks off. Kiwi turns, zipping his lips before walking away.

My body shakes as I stare after Kiwi, wondering if I just made the biggest mistake of my life.

Tobias

An elbow connects with my face, jerking me awake as well as causing me to reach under my pillow where my gun lays. My eyes barely adjust to the dark before I'm blinking at what the fuck just hit me.

"No...." someone whimpers. My eyes drop down to Gabriel lying next to me, only instead of him sleeping peacefully, he's twisting around.

"Little Rabbit?" I mumble, pushing the gun back under my pillow. "Gabriel...."

"NO!" he screams, tears streaming down his face, sobbing for reasons I don't know. "I'm sorry, I'm sorry. Please... leave HER ALONE!" he yells, fists flying.

Unsure of what to do, I drag his body on top of mine, holding him against my chest. "Gabriel. Come on, wake up," I murmur into his ear, rubbing circles onto his cheek, trying my best to calm him down. I vaguely remember having night terrors when I was little. It took me years to get over them.

"I'm right here, Little Rabbit. I'm here," I croak, my throat closing from emotions I'm not ready to deal with.

His body tenses; his breathing stops before he struggles against my hold.

"Let me go," he snaps, clawing at my skin.

"Little Rabbit, it's me, baby, it's me," I mutter, hating that he's fighting against me, thinking I'm going to hurt him.

"T–Tobias?" He stops fighting against my hold.

"It's me, it's me."

Gabriel shifts, turning his body, and wrapping his arms around my neck. His hot tears hit my neck, trailing down. Tightening my hold on him, I ease us down until he's lying on top of me.

We lay there for what feels like hours, fully expecting him to be asleep until he starts mumbling into my ear. "I grew up in a motorcycle club. They used to beat me and my sister. Izel, she got the worst of it. I'm talking... they raped her, they...he told our father that we were running away. We were caught, and when.... When it happened, they took her to the basement for a week. I didn't see her; I thought they killed her. It was a few weeks after that, two of Dan's best friends.... They caught me snooping through Dan's office. They beat me, they were going to... they...."

"Names," I growl. I was going to hunt them down. I don't care how long ago it was, I didn't care. I was going to hunt them down and kill them all. Torture, and make the damn town run in their blood.

"Izel's boyfriend... well, husband now, he killed them. She was kidnapped after we ran. He found her and killed them all. Everyone...everyone but Dan."

"I'm going to finish him," I say, grabbing his face. I need him to see the sincerity of my words.

"I killed, Tobias," he whispers, his nose brushing against mine. "You don't scare me because I grew up in violence. I've been around it. I've killed before."

"I won't hurt you," I declare.

"I know you won't. I might be crazy, but I trust you," Gabriel mutters, pressing his lips against mine.

"I won't let anything happen to you," I whisper against his mouth. I might not be able to take revenge on those who hurt him, but now that he's mine, I won't let anyone get near him again.

I just barely fall asleep before my phone starts going off. Quickly grabbing it before it wakes Gabriel up, I answer.

"Da," I whisper.

"Office, we need to talk," Kyler says, hanging up the phone before I can say anything. Shifting Gabriel off of me the best I can, I grab my sweatpants and shirt from the floor before heading downstairs.

The moment I step inside, Kyler paces around my desk, glancing up when I close the door behind me.

"Better talk and talk fast," I snarl, walking around my desk, and sitting down.

"Someone else is stalking Gabriel," he states, handing me a large envelope. My left eye twitches, barely glancing at him before I'm tearing into the envelope. I'm not sure what I expect, but when I see pictures of him dating all the way back to his apartment, of me walking in and then him at his art studio, rage explodes through my body.

"I found this waiting on the doorstep. I had Nick look at all the cameras, and they've been cut. I called Killian to hack him into the feed, and there's nothing he can see. He's working with Aziza right now, but…. Here."

As if I didn't think this could get any worse, he hands me a note.

You took someone important from me. I'm going to take something important to you.

Flipping it over, nothing but those words are written. Nothing else, no name, not that I expect there to be. Who would leave their name behind unless they want to get caught?

"I'm going to take Gabriel to Salem's." I don't know where the idea came from, but now that the words are out, it sounds more and more like a better idea.

"You don't think we can protect him here?" Kyler asks.

"I do.… But with this and the fact someone got onto the property when he first arrived, I think going away, where no one but you and I know, it'll give us time to figure out who's after him."

"Whoever's after him is probably the same one who was leaking information about the shipments to Billy and his brother. We're still working on who they were working with."

Thinking about it, it makes sense. This person had to be giving Billy information about our shipments of weapons, allowing him to break in and steal from me. But the question begs, who is it? And why?

"When are you going to leave?"

"In the morning."

Kyler nods his head. "I'll arrange for a car."

"No, I'll take one of mine. I don't want to risk there being a tracker on it. I'll get in contact with Salem on the way, and text Aziza to make sure no one can trace the call. I want you to stay in the city. Keep your ears alert for anything. Dad, Mom, and Blake are coming into town in a few days. I'll have them meet us at Salem's."

"Dimitri's not going to like that."

Rolling my eyes, I can't help but chuckle. Ever since Salem and Zane met over seventeen years ago, Salem has been a thorn in my father's side. I'm not sure why he deals with it, but I can't help but think it's because he's scared of her. Even a part of me is terrified of the things she can do.

"Blakes coming to town?" Kyler laughs.

"I swear if something–"

"Dude, she's seventeen, and she's more like a little sister. We just like to rile you up."

Glaring over at my best friend, I watch his smile slowly fade in seconds. "I'll kill you."

"I k–"

"Kyler, I'll murder you. Slowly and very painfully, I will keep you alive as I remove your guts."

His eyes widen, and there's a slight tick in his jaw and a pull as he bites his inner cheek. I've never threatened him like this, but maybe he doesn't understand, even though my sister annoys me like any sibling would, she's my sister and I'll pull anyone's guts out that hurts her.

"Tobias, I'm not into your sister. I'm not a pedophile, and I'm hurt you would even think that. She's like a sister to me... you know, I never had a family...." Kyler's voice hardens, blinking away any emotion that was getting caught in his voice.

"I trust you," I tell him.

Kyler doesn't say anything, nodding before getting to his feet. "Let me know when you arrive," he says, opening the door and leaving me in my office.

Blowing raspberries, I shred the pictures of Gabriel before heading back upstairs. Thankfully, he's still asleep by the time I climb into bed. Throwing an arm around my waist, he rests his head on my chest. Only

I can't sleep, my mind racing over who it could be, and the ways I want to tear this world apart for him.

Only feeling like we just barely started and now everything is falling apart.

18

Gabriel

I shift onto my side, my eyes blinking open when I don't feel Tobias next to me. Did he leave me? Does he regret what we did? The memories of my night terrors, waking up and confessing some of my past to him last night rush in. Bolting up, I clench the blanket to my chest, doubt and fear clogging my throat, so I barely register when the bathroom door opens, and Tobias walks out, completely naked.

"Gabriel?" he asks, worry filling his voice. But I don't focus on that. Instead, I focus on the fact I finally opened up to someone about my past and now they're leaving me.

I open my mouth to tell him something, anything at this point, but nothing comes out. I can feel the panic ripping through my heart, threatening to wreck me.

"Gabriel!" Tobias snaps. All of a sudden, he's grabbing my throat again, bringing me back down. I can't understand why when his hand is wrapped around my throat I can't think clearly.

"I'm sorry," I whisper.

"Why are you running from me?"

"I'm not running," I lied. I was definitely thinking of running.

"Gabriel."

Biting my bottom lip, my eyes flick to the side, barely catching the duffle bag sitting in the corner, and the panic comes rushing back in. Tobias must have felt my pulse or he's just that good at reading people because he glances to where I'm looking.

"It's not what you think," he finally says, pushing me back on the bed. Crawling on top of me, he grabs my hands placing them above my head.

"And how do you know what I'm thinking?" I ask.

"You might think you're good at hiding what you feel but you're not. It's written all over your face, Little Rabbit. You thought I was leaving, and your mind was racing. It's all in your eyes."

"Stop fucking reading me," I snap.

"No."

"Fuck you," I spit, hating that he can read me so easily. I hate that he reads too well. No one but my sister is able to. And now that she's halfway across the country, it's not nice that no one can. No one until him.

"If that's what it takes."

I frown at his meaning until he shoves two of his fingers into my mouth. Being the slut that I am, I can't help the moan, sucking on his fingers.

"Leave your hands up there," Tobias orders, pulling his fingers from my mouth. Ripping the blanket down, I don't know how I didn't notice that I was naked, but my cock lays against my stomach, precum leaking from my tip.

Tobias grabs my thighs, pushing them against my chest.

"I can't be gentle," he whispers, his glorious cock stands out at me My breath hitches, remembering the piercings he has. The anticipation doesn't last long when he presses the tip against my hole. Leaning over he spits down on us. We both know it's not enough, but neither of us seem to care. Not when he presses forward, the tip of his cock pushing against the tight muscle of my ass. I bite down on my lip, blood dripping into my mouth.

"Fu–fuck," he hisses above me. "You're fucking tight."

I can't say anything. Between my ass already being sore from last night, and now him pushing into me, I can't speak, let alone breathe. The moment he breaks through that tight ring we both let out a groan.

"Gabriel?" Tobias whispers.

Realizing I must have closed my eyes, I snap them open, looking into Tobias's, the question written all over his face. Nodding my head, I say, "I'm okay. Keep going." I breathe, and moving back, I grab at his ass, pulling him forward.

Thankfully, he doesn't comment on the fact that I moved my hands or the fact I'm grabbing his ass and trying to move him forward. Instead, he pushes forward and doesn't stop until his hips meet my skin.

"Fuck, Gabriel," he hisses, pulling back before thrusting forward. Abruptly he grabs the back of my head, slamming our mouths together. His hips speed up, and our mouths turn from kissing to breathing against each other. Pushing my legs higher, holding them on his shoulders, Tobias thrusts forward pressing against my prostate.

"Oh god, oh fuck... To–Tobias," I shout. I can't form any more words. I can't do anything but hold on for dear life as he possesses every part of my body. Moving inside me like he owns me, *he does*. It takes no time for me to become a whimpering mess, begging for him to not stop, begging for everything. My inner muscles began to spasm. I know I'm going to cum, and I hadn't even touched my dick.

"I need you to cum, Gabriel. Cum for me," Tobias grunts above me, slamming his hips forward. I barely get a second to think before I'm doing as he orders, cum shooting from my dick between us, landing all over my stomach and some landing on him.

"Fuckkkkk." Tobias' hips jerk, his own cum releasing deep inside me. He drops his mouth to my neck, sucking on my skin as his climax rocks through him. Wrapping my arms and legs around his body, my fingers wrack through his hair, massaging circles against his scalp.

"I... are you hurt?" he finally asks, breathing against my throat.

"I'm perfect." I sigh, feeling content.

Pulling out of me, Tobias lies next to me, dragging my body to press against his side. Neither of us speak, our breathing finally evening out. I think he falls asleep until he says, "We're going on a trip."

Sitting up, I spin around, confused.

"What are you talking about?"

Tobias sighs, sitting up against the headboard. Grabbing the back of my neck, he gently massages circles into my skin. I think this is the gentlest he's ever been, and it raises all types of red flags.

"Someone's been stalking you."

A giggle escapes me. "Yeah, you, goofy."

Tobias shakes his head, his hold on my neck tightening. I don't know what's got him so freaked out, but the smile plastered on my face drops.

"You're serious... who?" I ask, trying to process what he's saying. My heart beats faster, nearly jumping from my chest. "I... I don't understand." They're all dead. No one should be after me. I can't breathe.

"Gabriel," Tobias says, grabbing my cheek. My eyes barely focus on him. Everything feels blurry, everything hurts. I can't go through it again. I can't, oh god, *I can't breathe, I can't fucking breathe.* "Look at me, Little Rabbit." His voice sounds so far away. Too far. "Gabriel, look at me!" his voice demands, no room for argument. "Focus on me."

Nodding my head, I bite my bottom lip, trying to hold back the tears. I already cried last night. I don't need to fall apart again.

"They're not after you," he says, dragging me further up his body until I'm lying across his chest. "They're after me and trying to hurt me by going for you. But I'm not going to let that happen." I open my mouth to protest, but Tobias shakes his head. "No, there's no room for argument. Not here, and not now. We're going to find out who these fuckers are. One of my aunts is already looking into it. And while we look, me and you, we're going on a trip."

"We're running," I blurt out, resting my forehead against him.

"I don't run, but if it protects you and keeps you safe, then that's what we're going to do. There's nothing in this world I wouldn't do for you, so we're going on this trip."

Pushing against his chest, I sit up, straddling his hips. If this was a different situation, I'd probably be more aware of the fact that we're both naked, and I'm not bothering to cover up.

"There's no place that's safe," I mutter, my fear wrapping around my throat. It's like I'm fifteen all over again, afraid for my life, not knowing if I'm going to wake up in the morning.

"Listen to me." Tobias sits up, pulling me forward so our chests are pressed against each other. "Where we're going, no one and I mean it, no one can touch you."

Biting my bottom lip, we stare at each other, feelings spinning around us, words that aren't spoken but still there. "Okay," I mumble, putting my life in his hands. "Don't break me."

"Never," Tobias says, pressing his lips against mine. His hands grab onto my back as if it's the only thing calming him down. And I don't know how I didn't even think about what he must be going through. I might not know much about the Mafia life, but I do know that they're ruthless, they're killers, and most of all they're not someone you want to mess with. And to know someone is threatening someone involved with the boss, I can't imagine.

Tobias pulls back, rubbing our foreheads together. "Come on, let's shower and get going. If we start now, I'm afraid I won't let you go until...well, never."

Smiling against his lips, I don't see a problem with that. But knowing that someone's after me, and someone's after Tobias, I nod before climbing off his lap, putting my trust in the fact that Tobias can protect me.

19

Gabriel

When Tobias said we were going on a trip, I had no idea we were going to the country. North Carolina to be exact. And of course, the fucker decides to drive through, only stopping when we need to. Sure, I take a fat nap for half of it. And when I ask if his family knows we are traveling he says no and barely speaks two words after. Thankfully, he gives me control over the radio, and much to his dislike I play Taylor Swift the entire time.

"For fucks sake," Tobias growls. Reaching across he turns the radio off, not sparing me a glance.

"What's your problem?" I hiss, folding my arms over my chest.

Tobias doesn't say anything, instead turning his blinker on before turning left onto a dirt road. I can't see anything due to it being dark—nothing but darkness, the gravel road, and a fence keeping the road separate.

"I'm assuming this is it?" I ask, leaning forward.

"Yeah," Tobias mutters.

It takes a minute before the headlights shine onto a two-story farmhouse. As we slowly approach, two SUVs and pickup sit off to the side, and there's a wraparound porch, with large, open windows. It's beautiful and reminds me a lot of Zion and Izel's house.

Tobias pulls over next to the other vehicle before parking and turning it off. Glancing at me, I think he's going to say something before he's shuffling out of his seat and walking around the car. Opening my door, he frowns when he reaches me.

"I was going to open that for you," he mutters.

"I.... I'm sure Mafia bosses don't open other people's doors." I chuckle, trying to lighten the mood.

"I want, never mind." Tobias shakes his head. Turning around he heads for the house, but I don't like that. Grabbing at his arm, I pull him back, realizing I'm probably the only one who's ever touched him like this and lived.

"Please don't walk away from me."

"I like doing things for you. I don't... I don't want you to just think of me as the Mafia boss. I want to be normal. I... don't be afraid of me because of who I am."

"I'm not." it's the truth. I don't think I've ever been scared of him, and I don't think there is anything he could do that would make me scared of him.

"Here." Looking down, Tobias holds out my phone.

"I thought..." I frown, unsure if I should take it or not.

"Take it, Gabriel. I trust you."

Slowly taking my phone, I shove it into my pocket, not bothering to look through it.

"Come on, let's go meet my aunt and uncle," Tobias says, grabbing my hand.

Leading me up the stairs, Tobias doesn't knock before opening the door and dragging me along.

"Shouldn't you have... knocked?" I whisper. Clenching his hand in mine, the whole house is plunged into so much darkness that I have no idea how he can even see two feet in front of him.

"No, knowing Salem she'd probably punch me for knocking when I can simply just walk in." Tobias leads me through the living room, holding onto my hand, though I'm sure he must be grossed out from the amount of sweat my hand has on it. And when we round the corner, my heart might as well drop from my chest, when I take in the guy, I'm assuming is his uncle. He's huge—not as big as Zion, thank fuck, because no one should ever be that big. His strong gaze locks onto mine immediately. He frowns, and my eyes can't leave his. I feel nauseous, and the panic quickly returns.

"Uncle Zane, knock it off," Tobias growls, dragging me further into the room. That doesn't stop this Zane guy from giving me a murderous stare that has me dragging my feet and shrinking behind Tobias.

"Zane." A feminine voice appears behind us, causing me to jump about three feet in the air. "Hello, Tobes." Nudging into his back, I watch as a girl, who's literally just as small as my sister steps forward. Her medium-length black hair is tied into a braid going down her back, with overalls and a flannel, speaking true to the whole farm situation.

"Aunt Salem, Uncle Zane, this is Gabriel."

"Hello, Gabriel." Salem smiles towards me, while Zane narrows his eyes even more if that's even possible.

"Uncle Zane, don't be such a bitch," Tobias growls, pulling me closer. I would never get over his possessive side.

"I don't think that's possible." Salem laughs, setting down a plate of something, I wasn't too sure what it was. "The first time I met Zane he whined because I hit him with a bat." Shrugging her shoulders, she steps towards the fridge.

"I don't remember that," Tobias says, dragging me towards the island. He leans forward, taking a piece of the bread and putting it onto my plate before taking one for himself.

"You were just born." Salem once again shrugs, handing him a tub of butter.

"What is this?" I whisper to Tobias.

"Banana bread. Salem made it when she kidnapped me." Zane smirks over at her.

"I did not kidnap you. I saved your damn life and then decided to try and make you feel at home with some baked goods," she says, waving a butter knife at him. Zane doesn't look afraid. Instead, he's smiling at her with love in his eyes.

"You're right," Zane mumbles, finally drawing his eyes away from her.

"Tobias kidnapped me," I blurt out. I regret it the moment the words leave my mouth. But what makes me regret it even more is when Zane's eyes snap to mine and then Tobias, while Salem holds a better grip on the knife and glares at Tobias. I worry for a moment that she might try and stab him.

"He's lying." Tobias takes a bite of banana bread.

Now, I should probably agree, let them all think it's a joke. But what comes out of my mouth is, "No, I'm not. You literally took me in the middle of the night. And that was after you were stalking me for a month." A few things happen all at once. Zane chuckles, and Tobias glares daggers at me moments before Salem moves around the island and punches Tobias.

"Dude, what the fuck!" Tobias growls, standing his ground in front of her.

"Tell me you're lying. Tell me you didn't kidnap him!" she hisses, still holding onto that butter knife.

Tobias is too silent, and I don't like it.

"Tobias, you better run for it," Zane mutters, shoving the stupid banana bread into his mouth.

"I thought at least your mother would've taught you better! You can't just kidnap people, Tobias! It's wrong, let him go," Salem hisses, peeking around Tobias' shoulder and she looks directly at me. "Honey, you can leave. Zane will take you to the bus station and give you some money. Go home and forget about this ungrateful little shit. He'll be dead in a moment anyways." Once more narrowing her eyes at Tobias, she goes to take a step towards him.

Grabbing him around the waist I pull him back, placing my hand on his hip.

"Thank you, but I don't need you to do that," I finally say.

"He kidnapped you."

"And stalked me, and violated me, and much more. But I... well...." I can't finish my sentence. I barely know these people, and to tell him I loved waking up to his come on my mouth might sound a little odd.

"He wants me as much as I want him," Tobias finishes for me.

"You're gay?" Zane asks.

Snapping my head towards him, I'm moments from ripping him a new ass. But I'm surprised when there's no hint of disgust. Only that he's actually interested in Tobias and if he's gay or not.

"No," Tobias answers, pressing his butt against my leg.

"So... you're bisexual then?" Salem asks, going to stand near Zane.

"No."

They both look confused, passing a look at each other. I almost laugh when Tobias finally moves away and sits back down next to me.

"I'm confused," Salem mutters, creasing her brows, glancing between us.

"What is there to be confused about? I'm not gay or bisexual."

"But are you guys like together?"

They look at me to answer, but I refuse. I don't know what Tobias and I are. Are we dating? Just fucking? I'm not sure. But thankfully, I don't have to answer or wait for long before Tobias answers them.

"Yes. I just said he wants me as much as I want him." Tobias finishes the bread on his plate, draining the rest of his whiskey before standing. "We're going to bed," he says, grabbing my hand and pulling me from my chair.

"Uh, it was nice meeting you two!" I yell as Tobias drags me up the stairs.

I stare at the dark ceiling waiting for Tobias to come back in from grabbing our bags from outside. My brain searches for who could be after Tobias, but of course I come up blank because I have no clue what it's like in his world. I have no idea what this means, none of it. Tobias just told them we're dating, but that's news to me. I have no idea how to process him in general. Everything seems to be racing by while I'm rooted to the ground.

I'm too lost in thought to realize when Tobias enters and drops our bags off. It's not until he's grabbing at my hand, pulling me up from the bed, that I realize he's there. "Come, Little Rabbit."

Guiding me out the door and across the hall, he flicks the lights on before closing the door. My eyes slowly adjust to the brightness, taking in the medium-sized bathroom. Tobias drops my hand, leaning over the bathtub to the shower. Turning it on, the steam slowly begins to fill the room, fogging the mirror up.

Turning around he doesn't spare me a glance before he's pulling his shirt over his head. My eyes are glued to his dusky nipples, the urge to lick them—

"You keep looking at me like that and I'm going to have a hard time keeping my hands off you." Tobias breaks into my thoughts.

"I... I can't help it."

"Come on, let's shower. It's been a long drive and I just want to shower and crawl into bed."

Nodding, I agree. Shucking off my shirt, we both pull our pants down, breathing heavy. Glancing down, Tobias' cock sticks out, hard and proud.

"Fuck," I mutter under my breath.

"Gabriel."

"Yes?"

"Shower, now," he growls.

Yanking me forward, he drags me into the shower. Neither one of us speaks. Instead, we fall into washing each other, his fingers digging into my scalp. Turning the water off, we dry off, brush our teeth, and climb into bed. Lying next to each other, I think he's asleep, but when a question pops into my head, I can't stop but want to ask.

"Are you awake?" I ask, turning my head towards him.

"Hmmm?"

"You know I have a question," I say, rolling over to lie on Tobias's chest.

"You always do," he mutters.

"How did you know I was a bottom? I could have been a top."

"You're not," he states.

"You don't know that." He couldn't. I could very well give off a top vibe.

"Yes, I do." Tobias smiles, closing his eyes as if this conversation is done. Which is not true, it's just getting started. Because there's no way he would know unless...

"How do you know?" I ask, raising up until I'm inches from his face.

"We're not talking about this right now, Gabriel. It's in the middle of the night."

"I want to know. So you're going to tell me, love." I smile sweetly the moment his eyes pop open. And they only open because I called him "love." His favorite nickname. He wasn't a fan of the other ones.

Tobias sighs, closing his eyes again. "You like that blue dildo the most."

I couldn't be hearing him correctly. There's no way. Before he kidnapped me, I used my favorite dildo, the biggest one I owned, ten inches, wide base, and a little curve at the tip. I used it *every night.* So the only way he would know is if....

"You didn't," I growl.

Tobias, of course, doesn't say anything and just lies there, eyes closed and relaxed.

Fucker.

"How many nights?" I ask sitting up. When he doesn't say anything, I reach over, pinching his left nipple, hard.

"OW! Jesus H Christ! What is wrong with you!" Tobias yells, smacking my hand away from his now hopefully bruised nipple.

"Should've bitten it," I hiss.

"Keep running your mouth and I'm going to use it for something else," Tobias growls right back.

"I wouldn't, I might bite the tip off!" Snatching the blanket off him, I roll to the side of the bed, irritated and frustrated but most of all turned on. I shouldn't be turned on by him, but my body doesn't care when it comes to Tobias. Only that I now want his pierced cock inside my ass while I suck on my blue dildo.

"Gabriel," Tobias calls, grabbing my shoulder. Yanking my arm away from him, I slam my eyes closed. Feeling childish, but I don't care.

"What makes you madder, the fact I watched you..." he whispers, his hand slipping down and palming my junk. "Or that I jacked off to you without you knowing." Biting on my earlobe I can't help the gasp or moan that leaves my mouth, damn him. "I watched you for months, jacking off to you shoving that dildo into your ass, listening to your moans." Removing his hand, I whimper when I hear him suck his finger into his mouth before spreading my ass cheek apart and circling my hole. "Sometimes you'd bend over and give me the most perfect view of your hole, and sometimes you'd sit on it." I hiss the moment his finger breaches my muscles, only to relax when his tongue licks the column of my neck. "I watched you jack off, moaning and screaming out. Begging someone to fuck you hard."

Suddenly he's ripping his hand from my ass and turning me onto my back, pressing me against the mattress with his weight. Tobias spreads my legs apart, settling between them.

"You'd beg and beg for it to be harder," he continues, reaching into the bedside table. I don't catch what he grabs, only the flick of a bottle before I feel the familiar tip against my ass.

"It turned me on the most when you'd fuck one dildo and then suck on another one. I don't think I came harder in my life until I watched you do that.... Well, maybe that's a lie." He laughs against my shoulder blade before I feel the tip of the dildo breaches my hole. I clench my cheeks. "Relax, Little Rabbit. Let me take care of you," Tobias whispers, pushing it into my body. Relaxing, I close my eyes. Flourishing in the feeling of being full. It might not be Tobias, but the feeling is all the same. It feels exactly like his.

Tobias growls in my ear the whole time he's fucking me with the dildo. And I can't help the sounds that leave my mouth.

"More," I beg. "Love...give me more." I want his cock in my mouth. I'm drooling, needing him to fuck my mouth while I'm stuffed full of the dildo.

"What do you want, Little Rabbit? Use your words," he murmurs back. And I hate him for it. I hate that he knows exactly what I want. But he's going to make me say it. "Come on, say it." Twisting the dildo, he pulls it almost all the way out before pushing it roughly back in.

"Fuck me! Fuck my mouth!" I scream, pushing back against his hand.

"Good boy." Tobias laughs. I'm moved from lying on my stomach to my back all of a sudden, my head hanging off the bed. All the while Tobias stands in front of me, gripping the back of my thighs, still plunging the toy into me. "Open," he demands, gripping his cock.

Gladly, I kiss his crown before sucking him into the back of my throat, gagging when the piercings tickle my throat.

"Good boy," he praises, pulling out of my mouth before thrusting back in. "Be a good boy for me and keep that mouth open."

I nod around his cock, drool running down my chin. But I don't care. Between him fucking my face as if it was my ass and plunging the toy into my actual ass, I'm losing my mind.

I'm so close to coming from this alone, my cock hurts. I can feel my balls swelling, and the need to touch myself is almost overwhelming.

"That's it, take my cock," Tobias growls. His balls hit my face, his cock buried in my throat while he twists the toy in me. I explode, screaming around his dick. Tobias' mouth is suddenly licking my stomach, pulling the toy from my body as he erupts into my mouth. Coming down my throat, I drink him down happily. Loving his taste, loving his groans, and simply just... loving him.

"Fuck..." he curses, popping out of my mouth. "I lied. I think that is the hardest I've ever come before."

Throwing my head into the mattress, blood no longer rushing to my brain, I laugh.

Tobias smiles down at me, hands on hips, standing naked and proud before kissing me.

I try not to think about what's going to happen when he lets me go because I don't want to. I want to stay with him and never leave. Only hoping he'll love me as much as I love him.

20

Gabriel

"Has he always been this grumpy?" I whisper to Salem.

Tobias sits on the floor in front of me. I'm not entirely sure why he felt the need to sit on the floor, there's plenty of space to sit on the couch or the other two chairs in this living room. But no. Instead, he sits in front of me, my legs over his shoulders, while he rubs my feet.

"Not until his teens." She shrugs, smiling down at him. I might not know Tobias or Salem that well, but just looking at them I can see a bond. I want to ask but Salem also doesn't seem like the type of person you can just ask. I can tell she's a person who likes to keep secrets. Which is fine by me. I have them as well.

Keeping my mouth shut, I turn my attention back towards *Mulan* and try to focus on the movie. But I can't. I can't focus, not when Salem and Zane keep stealing glances at each other. And not when Tobias is peeling my sock off and rubbing circles into my heel. I am not a foot guy, they're gross and men always have crusty, hairy toes. But for some reason, Tobias is suddenly making me a liar because of the way he's spending time massaging each of my toes. Working his palm into my heel and for fucks sake, I can barely stand this any longer.

"Kitten...." Zane's voice breaks through my sexual tension. Right, we're watching a movie, I should be focusing on that.

"Let's go see Pumpkin." I have no idea who Pumpkin is, but I could cheer when Salem doesn't say anything, just grabs Zane's hand and they're out the door.

Turning my head back towards the TV, I open my mouth to say something, anything. But the words are lost in my throat when Tobias' hot tongue licks from my heel all the way down to my toes.

"Fuck..." I gasp, unable to stop myself. I promise, I'm not a foot guy. I'm not. I just seem to be with Tobias licking and sucking on them. "Love..." I groan, the words getting caught in my throat when Tobias is up off the ground and hovering over me.

"Kiss me," he demands. Not letting me refuse or tell him I want to, he fuses our mouths together, slipping his tongue into my mouth. I hate that he always demands that I kiss him. He shouldn't have to demand me to do anything. Why doesn't he realize I'll do anything for him? He can kiss me whenever he wants.

But I don't say anything. Instead, I let him take over our kiss. His tongue moves along with mine, dominating me in the best ways, in the ways he knows how to. One of his hands presses against my throat, restricting my air, while he grinds his hips against my leg. His cock is hard, painfully hard. The feeling of his piercing pressing against my thigh causes me to shiver.

Suddenly, Tobias rips his mouth away from me, gripping my throat, breathing heavily and searching my face for what I'm not sure.

"I didn't kidnap you."

I'd probably frown if it weren't for the lack of air, but it was impossible with Tobias' hands pressing against my throat, squeezing and then letting go. He was fighting something inside his head, and I doubted he would tell me what was troubling him so much.

I don't get a warning before he's letting my neck go and ripping my sweatpants, boxers down my leg.

"Wh–AH," I hiss the moment Tobias warm mouth wraps around my crown, sucking my entire length down his throat. Gagging, he keeps my cock in the back of his throat, locking eyes with me. *Fuck.* He looks so good with my dick in this mouth.

"Turn around," he sneers, popping off.

Twisting around, knees on the couch, I glance back just in time as Tobias grabs my hips pulling my ass back.

"Tobias," I groan.

"Yes, Little Rabbit?" he asks, leaning over my back. His lips latch onto the back of my neck, sucking and licking.

"Fuck... I–fuck, your family is right there," I hiss when his warm, large hand wraps perfectly around my length. His aunt and uncle could literally walk in at any moment, but I can't bring myself to care. I want, *need,* him inside me.

"I bet you're needy," he whispers along my jaw, nipping at my skin. "I bet your hole is ready for my cock. Open nice and wide for me."

"Tobias," I groan, needing him to stop talking about fucking me and to just get it on.

"Yes, Little Rabbit?" Why this man instinctively teases me, I will never understand. But I can't lie about loving it.

I don't get a chance to say anything before he presses the tip of his finger against my hole, circling, and taunting me. I don't get a chance to beg him or plead before he's pushing forward and stuffing me full of his thick finger. My ass clenches, a strained moan leaving my lips.

"You look so fucking good with my finger shoved in your ass. The way your hole fits my finger so well, I bet it would fit my cock even better," he growls, yanking my head back by my hair. Our eyes connect the same angry eyes that I once thought meant he was pissed at me for something I didn't know I did. Only to learn that he's not angry, in fact, he just craves me—craves my body and the way it reacts to him.

I whimper at the loss of his finger. I don't think he understands how much I truly need him inside me.

"Hmm, such a slut," he murmurs, dragging his tongue across my jaw over my lips. My eyes begin to flutter closed. It's then he aggressively shoves his tongue into my mouth. It's sloppy and fierce, but I love it. "Fuck," he hisses pulling back. My lips chase after him, not wanting to let his mouth go for one second. "Not only is your hole needy for me, but so is your mouth. So, fucking needy," he whispers against my mouth. "Is your cock needy for my mouth again? I should make you beg for it. Imagine that you're on your knees, crawling to me. Begging for my cock, begging to be filled. You'd be a good boy and take all my cum, wouldn't you? You'd swallow it all like a good boy."

I'm nodding my head before I even realize it. Anything to be his good boy. Fuck, I'd give him a kidney if that's what he wanted.

Suddenly I'm being lifted, my pants thrown to the ground before Tobias sits down settling me on his knees. Not looking away once, Tobias unzips his pants taking his delicious cock out. I whimper, needing it in me right now.

Grabbing my cock, he presses them together, a strained hiss escaping my mouth when he starts stroking us together. Tobias' eyes darken, his breathing picking up as he glances down at my weeping cock. I can't wait for it anymore. Ripping his hand away, I climb further up, reaching around and I place the head of his cock at my hole. Baring down, his cock and piercings splitting me open burns, but I don't stop until I'm seated back on his thighs.

"F-fuck, Gabriel," Tobias hisses, his hands gripping my hips. Smiling down at him, I plant my feet on the couch, my hands on his chest. Pushing up, I slam back down.

"*Fuck!*"

"Shhh, love," I mumble, trying my darndest to not cry out either, but he feels too good. "We don't want your family to come in here thinking I'm violating you," I smirk when his eyes pop open, glaring up at me.

"Keep that smart mouth up and I'm going to stuff it full."

"Yeah? And how do you plan to do that with my ass stuffed with your co—"

Tobias cuts me off, shoving three fingers into my mouth. Using one hand he holds my ass up, thrusting up. My moans are garbled, drool running down my chin and his wrist.

"Look at you, taking my cock so good," he mumbles, his fingers stretching my mouth wide, his cock pounding into me. I can't even imagine what I look like, but I couldn't care less either. Not when Tobias' eyes darken, his hand leaving my mouth, grabbing onto my length.

"To-Tobias," I whimper.

"You can take it, Little Rabbit. That ass was made to take my cock. So that's exactly what you're going to do. Take me like the good little slut you are. Make me cum in your ass," he growls. Spitting on my tip, he rubs his hand over the head before pumping faster. Between his dirty mouth, his dick inside me, and the way his large hand covers most of me, I am going to cum. A lot faster than I would like.

"I'm gonna cum," I whisper, my breath ragged. I can barely hold back, so the moment Tobias yanks me forward, our mouths fused together, I'm cumming into his hand, my ass clenching around his length causing his own release to shoot inside me. Tobias' hips slowly relax, a sigh leaving his lips into my mouth.

"We... we should clean up," I mumbled, remembering the fact that Salem or Zane could walk in at any second. I don't think they'd appreciate us banging on their couch.

When Tobias doesn't say anything, I risk glancing down. I hate how hard he is to read sometimes as if he's trying his hardest to hide any feelings or emotions.

"Love?" I whisper, my hands cupping his neck. "What's wrong?"

"Nothing, let's go." Lifting me off his lap, he stuffs his softening dick back into his pants, leaving me there confused on the couch over what the fuck just happened.

21

Gabriel

Tobias didn't speak at all during dinner, not when Salem or Zane tried talking to him or when one of the handlers that helped around the farm came over. It was quick after he disappeared into the room, and I found him sleeping in bed. I racked my brain trying to think of why Tobias just decided to leave me naked on the couch. I barely got myself together before Salem and Zane had walked back inside. Of course, Salem had a knowing look.

"Gabriel?" Salem mumbles, walking into the kitchen. "What are you doing up?" she asks, grabbing a coffee cup.

Glancing at the clock, I'm not surprised when I read four eighteen.

"I uh, haven't gone to bed," I whisper. Holding my own coffee, I take a sip, needing to hide in shame. I shouldn't be upset or embarrassed that the man I'm falling for is being a complete ass to me.

"He still not talking to you?"

I shouldn't be surprised that she noticed his bad attitude. She probably knows more about him, and the realization makes a pit in my stomach. I shouldn't be bothered. But the fact that he has a hard time opening up to me, I hate it.

Shaking my head, I basically down the rest of my coffee as Salem stares at me and continues to even as she fixes her cup of sugar with a hint of coffee.

"I can't help if I don't know what happened?"

"I don't know."

"What happened before he shut down?"

My cheeks heat, and I can feel the embarrassment clawing at my skin. When Salem smirks, I don't even have to ask to know she always knows the truth.

"I'm not talking about how y'all violated my couch. Which for your information I have cameras everywhere, and I mean *everywhere.*"

I swear if the ground could swallow me whole right here, right now, that would be my saving grace. My lungs fail, and my heart speeds up. If she has cameras, that means she must have seen...

"Zane told me. I didn't see anything if that's what you're worried about," Salem smirks, sipping her coffee.

I don't relax, I'm not sure what's worse if Salem caught or us the fact Zane *did.*

"Can I tell you a little bit about Tobias?" she asks, leaning against the kitchen island. I may not have known Salem for long, but since the moment I met her, I know I wouldn't want to get on her bad side.

Nodding my head, I hold my empty coffee cup, willing whatever she's about to tell me doesn't freak me out and cause me to have a panic attack.

"I assume you know he grew up in the Mafia. His father is the Pakhan, his mother was somewhat kidnapped but also saved by his father."

"Yeah, uh, he told me after we were attacked," I mumble.

"He was loud, outgoing, and free spirited. When he was around ten, he saw his best friend getting beaten by his father. Tobias knew what his own father did, but he also knew that his father didn't go after children and women. He has somewhat of a code he lives by, and when he found his friend being hurt by one of his father's soldiers, he freaked out. He told me what happened, and well, I took care of him. But Tobias saw too much at too young of an age to understand that things happen behind closed doors that Dimitri, his father, didn't know about. Tobias had a hard time accepting his father after that, and while he knew he was going to eventually take over for him, he also lost touch with reality. Tobias holds himself accountable for more than he should, and when every little thing goes wrong, even if it's not his fault, he takes it out on himself."

"What friend are you talking about?" I dare to ask. I have a feeling I know who he's talking about.

"His enforcer."

Kyler.

"I don't think he likes me that much," I blurt out. My eyes widen when I realize what I just said. Kyler never says much to me, but I can see the glares he gives me.

"Dimitri doesn't like me. In fact, he tried killing me a few times, but that's a different story, for another time. The point is, it doesn't matter if the others don't like you. Tobias isn't going to let any of them hurt you, even if it's his best friend. Right now, I think he's just working on accepting the fact he's into men and coming out to his father is racing through his head. But the fact he came out to Zane and me, and he didn't hold back...it's a good first step." Salem smiles wide at me.

"Has Kyler hurt you?" Suddenly Tobias is at my side, gripping my chin possessively. Everything fades away; the air between us thickens. I hadn't even realized he was here until now.

Shaking my head, Tobias tightens his grip.

"Enough of that bullshit. I asked you a question. You're not one of my men who do as they're told without question. You're a part of me and being a part of me means you question every little thing I do. It means my men respect you like they do me, and if they don't, do you know what happens?"

I start to shake my head when he growls low in his throat.

"No," I whisper, nervously racking my brain on what he's going to say.

"I'll kill them. I don't care who it is, I'll rip them apart, bathe in their blood. I don't care if it's my best friend, my father, any of them. You come first. You will always come first."

I'm shaking my head, denying any of the words he's saying to me. There's no way he can care for me that much. I'm no one, I'm nothing.

"Stop shaking your head." I twist from his grip, nearly falling backwards off the bar stool. "I... I need some air." I spin around, once again nearly tripping over my own feet.

"Gabriel!" Tobias shouts at me.

I don't listen, racing through Salem's house. I don't bother grabbing shoes or my coat. It's not that cold. I have no idea what I'm doing, or where I'm even going. But I can't face him. I'm not ready for him to know my worst fear. I'm not ready to see his face when I tell him and I'm surely not ready to lose him.

"Gabriel! Get back here right now!" I hear Tobias somewhere behind me.

"Just give me some time!" I scream back.

I don't hear if he says anything. I break out into a jog. I need to get away. I can't be here, and I can't be what he wants. He's the Pakhan for the damn Mafia. That's not me.

"For fucks sake," I vaguely hear him curse.

Oof.

I'm hit from behind. My arms attempt to block my face from hitting the ground, but I don't get the chance.

"Fuck," Tobias grunts. My eyes peel open, and I hit Tobias' intense glare, realizing he tackled me but must have twisted so he'd hit the ground and not me. "Hold on... let me catch my breath." Tobias pants, his eyes barely open.

"You wouldn't be out of breath if you didn't chase me," I growl. Placing my hands against his chest, I push off.

"Stop running away," he hisses, snapping his eyes to me.

"I'm not running per se. I..I– well, I was just trying to get some air," I lie. And from the death glare Tobias is shooting me, he knows I'm lying. I barely get to my feet, before Tobias is on his, hovering over me. His hands fist at his sides as if he has to physically fight himself not to reach out to me.

"Why are you running from me?" Tobias finally asks.

"I told you I'm not running," I lie again. I'm not sure why I can't just tell him the truth. But the idea of this all being one big joke to him... Or worse, what if he realizes I'm not enough for him? That he'd rather marry and love a girl, one that can give him children.

"Want to try telling me the truth?"

"Not really," I whisper, closing my eyes, willing the tears to go away. I don't deserve him; I don't deserve any of this. Tobias has done nothing but be kind and sweet towards me. I don't even have a reason to be acting the way I am. It's just that little voice inside my head.

"Gabriel Hollow, look at me when I'm fucking talking to you!" he yells.

Blinking my eyes open, a tear slips through. Cursing at my stupid self, I hate the way his eyes soften when he notices.

"Gab–"

"Don't. Please, just don't. I don't deserve you being kind or sweet or any of that. Please just... Call my sister, tell her to come get me, or better yet, can you just drop me off at some bus station? I should get out of your hair, I should... I need to leave." I know I'm rambling, not making any sense. I caught feelings, deep feelings for one that doesn't feel the same. "Don't say anything, just nod your head that you agree. I can't take your rejection, not right now."

"Will you shut up," he hisses.

Shaking my head, I swallow my hiccups, humiliation clawing at my skin. I hate everything about this. I never should have let him continue to break into my apartment. I never should have allowed myself to get this wrapped up in him.

I don't plan to witness him laughing at my expense. Stepping around Tobias, I don't get two feet before his arms are wrapping around me.

"Tobias—get off me!" I growl, sounding more like a wounded kitten than anything. "Get off me. Get off me. GET OFF ME!" I chant over and over. My body shakes, tears stream down my face, and the more I stand here in his arms fighting against his hold, the more I realize I have no idea why I'm fighting against him. I'm blowing a small problem out of the water, and now that I'm here, all this fighting is going to sound dumb.

"I'm not letting you go until you've calmed down."

I hiccup, trying to calm my breathing down, but I'm so worked up that my vision begins to blur, memories of Dan threatening to take me under.

"Absolutely not, you're not going back there. You're right here with me, Little Rabbit, and you're not going anywhere. You're going to take a deep breath—come on, with me."

Following through, his hand spreads across my chest, holding me still against him. He breathes in, following suit with me. Mumbling soft words to me, my eyes stay closed as he helps to calm my breathing down.

"Now tell me, what has you so worked up?" he whispers into my ear, his hand still rubbing against my chest, while the other holds me around my waist.

"It's... it's stupid," I murmur, afraid that the moment I tell him, he'll laugh and shove me away.

"Nothing inside that pretty little head is stupid. I don't care what it is, nothing too small or too big will have me walking away from you."

"I'm not enough for you," I blurt out before I think much about it.

"What are you talking about?" He spins me around, his jaw ticking. The heat in his eyes makes me squirm.

"Come on, Tobias, you're not stupid. When are you going to realize that I'm not enough? I mean your fathers going to want you to have children to carry on the legacy. Well, news flash, love, I have a dick. I can't give you children. When are you going to realize that you're not gay and I was just something to pass the time? You were bored, and you got the gay man to fall for you. I mean, come on Tobias, I'm not made for the hard life of the Mafia. I dealt with enough bad things growing up. I... I can't be what you want or need." I sigh, tears filling my eyes again. "I can't do this, Tobias. I fell. I fell so hard that I can't breathe without you. I can't move without you."

Tobias doesn't move or speak as I vomit my feelings. I hate when he gets like this, and when I think he's not going to say anything Tobias shakes his head. Stepping forward, he grabs the belt loop of my pants, yanking me forward.

"You don't get it," he whispers, grabbing my chin.

"Get what?"

"That heart inside your chest, that beating organ." He taps my chest, and letting go of my chin, he grabs the back of my neck. "It's that muscle in your chest that really has me possessed." Tobias wipes my cheek with his other hand. Bringing his thumb to his mouth, I suck in a breath when he moans and smirks down at me. "Hmm, tastes like mine."

Suddenly his hand wraps around my neck. "Don't you ever doubt my feelings for you again. I'm usually not into spanking but that doesn't mean I won't lay you across my lap and make that ass red before I fuck it."

I suck in a breath, a smile spreading across my lips. My emotions wreck my brain. I know I should fight him harder on this, but I know deep down he means everything he's saying. Tobias never once has said something he doesn't mean. I don't know why he would start now.

"Why did you shut me out?" I whisper, my hands dragging up his sides.

Tobias sighs, closing his eyes, his grip loosening around my throat. I don't like that. Tobias is hard around all edges, and I want his hand pressed against my throat. Controlling me the only way he knows how. So I do the only reasonable thing by jumping onto him. I swing my legs around his waist, wrapping my arms around his neck.

"You don't get to shut me out. If I get to question you, then you have to answer me. You don't want me clinging to you like a stage five clinger."

Tobias chuckles, his arms wrapping around my back holding me against his front.

"Who says I wouldn't mind a stage five clinger?"

"I'm talking I'll follow you everywhere. You won't ever shower alone; you won't even get to brush your teeth without me on your back."

"I wouldn't mind that," Tobias mutters, pressing his lips against mine.

"You say that now."

"I'll continue to say it. I wasn't lying when I said your heart is mine. It's been mine since I first laid my eyes on you, and it will continue to be mine. Even in death, I'll follow."

Shit, can this man make me cry even harder?

"I wasn't shutting you out earlier. I thought you didn't want them to see us together. When you said we should clean up, I thought you were hinting at us getting out of dodge so none of them saw us together."

I frown, his words slowly sinking in, and the more they sink in, the more the anger bubbles up. How could he just think that? I've tried to be all in, tried to bare my soul to him, but that's not true. He doesn't know everything, and as much as I don't want to tell him I need to.

"Gab–"

"No," I snap, wiggling, trying to get down from his hold.

"Stop," Tobias snaps.

Huffing, I sit back. If he's hell bent on holding me then he will have to hold my entire weight and if I fall, well, fuck him.

"I want to show you off. I want everyone to know, including my family, yours, everyone in *our* world. I don't want you to hide yourself, not from me and sure as fuck not from our family. So for the sake of my feelings, don't hide yourself. If you want to kiss me, kiss me, if you want a hug, hug me, and if you want to fuck, I'm your man."

My mouth opens and closes, gulping for air, because for fucks sake. When did Tobias become such a talker, and a smooth one at that?

"I...I– Tobias, I wasn't trying to hide us. I just didn't want to be seen naked; I don't want... the scars. I don't want them to ask questions, but I wasn't trying to hide from you or from them."

"Your scars make you who you are. And I could give two shits if they see us together, they're all going to know you're mine. I don't care what they think. I don't give two shits in the world, Gabriel," Tobias growls, slamming his lips against mine again. Everything he has he pours into our kiss, licking my mouth, demanding control over my mouth. But I can't give in to him, not knowing if he's going to let me in fully. He needs to trust me, needs to pick me.

"Tobias," I snap, breaking from his mouth. "Stop. Please, just..." Wiggling from his grasp, Tobias reluctantly lets me go, hands fisted at his sides. I know it must have been hard for him, but the idea of going on like we have been doesn't sit well.

"You have to let me in."

Tobias frowns, unsure of what I mean.

"I'm damaged, I'm broken, I have a missing part inside me. I'm a big clinger, and I'm not talking just about wanting to be near you. I'm talking about wanting to live in your skin. Rub your scent on me and never let me go. I'm obsessed with obsession. I don't want just the normal kind of love; I've seen that fall and break. I've seen it all. I want obsession. I want you so obsessed with me that you can't breathe when I'm not near you."

Shut up.

"Because I can't breathe without you. I want—no I need to be around you twenty-four-seven. I can't breathe if you're not in eyesight, and when you're not touching me. I hate it, I hate being away from you. I can't stand it." I sigh.

And worst of all the look he's giving me, I can't stand it. The emotionless, the no desire, the same desire that I hold for him. There's no fire in his eyes, and it makes this all worse. I'm baring my soul to him and he's standing there like he couldn't care less.

"Okay, well now that I've poured my heart out and you're just... Well, I'm going to go now." Biting my bottom lip, I blink, a tear slipping down my cheek.

"So you get to as you put it, pour your heart out, and I get nothing?" he snaps, glaring at me.

I open my mouth to say something, anything, but stop when Tobias starts to advance toward me.

"Shut up. It's my turn to talk."

Nodding, I hang my head, scared to look at him.

"Look at me!" he bellows.

He's a force to be reckoned with. My eyes immediately snap to him and the same fire that held my gaze not long ago is back. *As if I hold the moon.*

"You do." He answers the words I had no idea I even spoke out loud. Brushing his thumb across my cheek, I lean into his touch. "You make me a better man. And I don't say that lightly. Before you I was walking around the Earth, ready to burn it down to the ground because I had no path, no love, all I had was anger. Since I found you, all I've wanted to do is protect you from everything, from everyone. I want to wrap you in a bubble where you can't breathe without me. I want that obsession you want. I can't tell you how many nights I watched you sleep. I watched you every day and every night. Even when I knew it was wrong when I knew I should have let you go. But I couldn't, I couldn't live in a world where you weren't by my side. I knew what it meant for you to be a part of my life, and a stronger man would have walked away. But I can't, I won't. I'll tear this world apart for you, I'll burn it down. To worship at your feet is the biggest blessing I've ever had. I'm more than in love with you, Gabriel Hollow, more than obsessed. I won't live without you. You won't ever escape me. You won't live without me. I won't live without you."

My lungs explode, my heart aches, and the pain I feel is nothing compared to anything I've felt before. I want to crawl into his skin and live there. I want to wrap myself inside him and never let go.

"Tobias..." I started but have no idea what to even say. There are no words, nothing to say, so grabbing the back of his head, Tobias' eyes widen as I use the little strength I have and drag his lips down to mine.

He goes still, his mouth unmoving against mine. "Tobias...?" I sigh, the fear slipping in that he might not want this, even with the words he just spoke.

"You're it for me, Gabriel," he murmurs against my lips.

Nodding, I cling to his front. "You're all I want, you're all I need."

His arms wrap around me, lifting. Wrapping my legs around his waist, I pepper kisses along his neck and cheek. Needing him more than air, more than I need to fucking breathe.

"I need you," I whisper into his ear.

Tobias growls, his steps eating up the distance to the house. Somewhere in the back of my head I know I should stop this, wait until we're alone. Zane and Salem are somewhere in there and whatever we're about to do shouldn't be heard by others.

I don't stop whispering dirty things to him, kissing and licking along his neck. It's not until he kicks the door closed and drops me onto the bed that I take a moment to breathe.

"I want you," Tobias growls, stalking towards me.

"I need you," I mumble, my cock already painfully hard.

"No... I want you..." he says, scratching the back of his head. Cocking my head to the side I'm confused, and nothing would have prepared me for what he says next. "I want you to fuck me."

22

Tobias

I wasn't sure if I would ever want him inside me. I've accepted I'm bisexual, or at least for Gabriel, I am. But the more and more our relationship grows, the more and more I want to give him something no one has ever done before. I battled it for days, and when he finally had a breakthrough and confessed, he wanted obsession, something that I was already feeling, I wanted him more than I wanted to live. I wanted him inside me, whispering those dirty things to me. I wanted him to take my ass, even if I knew it was going to hurt. I didn't care. I wanted, needed, him.

"Tobias, we... we don't need to do this." He smiles, getting to his knees on the bed. I can see the firm outline of his cock, and it only matches mine, pressing against the zipper of my dress pants.

"I need this," I whisper, pulling his hips towards me. His eyes widen when he feels my own cock against his own, finally getting the idea that I need this. I want him.

"I should fight you on this, but the idea of finally owning this ass..." He giggles against my mouth, his hand grabbing a handful of my ass. I groan into his mouth, feeling my cock pulse, precum leaking from my tip. "Take your clothes off and lie on your back," he says, getting to his feet. Both of us strip off our clothes, and when I crawl onto the bed, I can see Gabriel stroking his cock, biting down on his bottom lip.

"You can back out any time, love," he says, crawling over my legs.

"I trust you." I only partly lie. I do trust Gabriel. He's the only one I would even consider doing this with. He's the only one I ever consider in this kind of way.

"You don't look so sure," he mutters, kissing his way up my chest, paying close attention when he gets to my nipple. Sucking it into his mouth, he bites down sending an electric jolt down my spine.

"Fuck..." I groan, cupping the back of his head. I've never been the needy one during sex, but with Gabriel, it's all different. I still love giving him the attention. I love making him scream for me. But I also love when he gives me soft touches, running his fingers through my hair. I love it all.

"Spread your legs for me, love."

I gulp, feeling like I just swallowed glass. But I do as he says, spreading my legs, letting him see a part of me that no other person has seen before.

"Tell me if you want me to stop," he whispers, kissing down my chest once more, swirling his tongue in my belly button before he nestles my cock. I desperately want to grab his face and shove my length down his throat. I know that will feel good, because I'm not so sure having Gabriel's tongue in my ass will.

"Tell me you understand. Tell me, love." Bossy Gabriel shocks me every single time. Whenever he gets that tone of voice, and tells me how it is, I'm always surprised. I shouldn't be. Gabriel has a wild mouth on him sometimes. But I love it.

"Yes, Little Rabbit," I mumble, my eyes dropping down to Gabriel's. Laying between my legs, he palms my cock, no pressure, but nonetheless, I'm struggling to breathe. He smiles, licking my tip, groaning when a little precum hits his tongue.

"Sh-shit." I hiss, my restraint of not shoving my cock into his mouth becoming nearly non-existent but yet quickly dies when he grabs my thighs and pushes them up.

Embarrassment hits me, my face surely turns red, and the breath in my lungs leaves. I have no idea if I was supposed to shave my asshole. Granted, I didn't expect this to happen tonight let alone Gabriel to want to eat my ass.

"Damn, Tobias." Gabriel breaks the silence. I hadn't realized I'd closed my eyes until he tightened his grip on my thighs, and I frowned at him. "Eyes on me. If I'm about to eat this virgin hole, then I expect you to watch," he growls.

"O–okay." My voice breaks.

"Okay, what?" he asks, cocking a brow at him. I wasn't sure if he wanted me to say sir or something else.

"Uh... okay... Little Rabbit."

"Good boy."

I squeak with disbelief at him calling me a good boy. But I never get the chance to comment on it before he's hooking my legs over his shoulders, spreading my cheeks apart, and running his flat tongue against my hole.

This shouldn't feel so good. But when he doesn't let up, running and working my ass open, I'm making noises I never thought I would. Gabriel hums against me, plunging his tongue into my ass. I reach down, palming my dick, needing some sort of relief. I don't get two strokes in before Gabriel rips his mouth from me, smacking my hand away.

Glaring down at him, he wraps his dainty fingers around my length. "No touching, this is mine, and when I'm eating your ass, I'm going to be the only one giving you pleasure," he hisses.

I nod my head in understanding. I'm weak when it comes to this man. I'm completely lost and needy for his touch.

My mouth parts and I pant when he licks my hole again, his hand giving my cock lazy strokes. I'm barely aware of his touch until a finger presses against me. I grit my teeth, my body tensing. I've never had anything inserted there before and I'm not sure how I like it.

"Love, relax for me." I try, but when his finger presses against my hole again, I'm tensing and biting my lip so hard I taste blood. "Tobias."

My eyes snap open, and I'm hit with so much emotion that it makes me uneasy. No one's ever dared to look at me like that, and now that I'm here, I don't want him to look at me any other way. I want all his love, and I want to be the only one who gets that love.

"I need you to relax for me. I'm not going to hurt you, I promise. Just relax and push out for me," he says with love.

Giving him a snarky nod, I take a breath through my nose and relax my muscles. All while Gabriel kisses my thigh, stroking my hard cock when he finally pushes the tip of his finger into my ass.

"Oh, fuck," I groan, my eyes nearly dropping closed when he thrusts his whole finger into me. Slowly my body adjusts to his finger, and I find myself moving my hips, wanting more.

"You look so good taking my finger, love," Gabriel praises, and I swear I'm moments from cumming. Especially when he hits something inside me that I half moan and squeal. "Fuck yes, you love that, don't you?" I have no idea what he's talking about, but when he hits it again, and his mouth engulfs my cock, I'm seeing stars. My hands cup the back of his head, forcing him further down my dick, his tongue lining up with my piercings.

"G–Gabriel," I croak. "I–I'm, fuck, I'm going to cum," I gasp, my knees growing weak. I can feel every pulse inside.

Gabriel barely pops off to mutter, "Cum," before sucking me back down his throat. The moment his finger pumps into me again, pressing against that sweet spot inside, I unload down his throat. I hear him swallow, his tongue licking up my slit before pulling his finger out.

It takes me longer than I'd like to admit before I'm able to open my eyes again, finding Gabriel smiling over at me. Getting to his knees, he slowly crawls up my body before laying his chin on my chest.

"You okay there, love?"

Eyes closed, I nod my head. I feel boneless and I know he hasn't even started yet.

"You look beautiful when you're flushed," Gabriel giggles, peppering my chest with kisses. Smiling, I blink my eyes open, amazed that I could feel so loved. "You know we don't have to do this."

"Stop trying to convince me. I want this, I want you." My voice shakes but my cock, still half hard, begs for another release.

"Good because I want you too." He presses one final kiss on my lips before grabbing my legs once more and hoisting them up against my chest. I flush even brighter, my hole out and open for him. I swallow, the lump refusing to leave my throat. "Fuck, you look.... Delicious, hmmm, delicious, and all mine."

"Gab–AH!" I cry out as his lips land directly on my puckered hole, sucking and his hot tongue plunging into me. "Oh my goooood." I yelp, my hands grabbing onto the back of his head as his finger travels up my thigh, pressing against my hole. I will myself to calm down, to breathe through my nose, but the slightest pressure has me tensing, my fingers digging into his scalp.

"Love, you need to relax. I need you to take a deep breath for me," Gabriel says against my ass. I nod even though I'm not sure if he can see me. "Words, darling, talk to me."

"Y–yes, I, fuck," I gasp when he slowly licks me again.

"Tobias."

"I understand, fuck, I understand."

Taking a deep breath, I relax my body, letting his finger slip into me. "Fucking hell," I groan, my fingers dragging into his hair. Gabriel peppers kisses along my thigh, sucking and licking along my skin. His finger sinks deeper and that noise I make shouldn't be normal, but I can't control it, and when he pulls out, before replacing it with two fingers. I'm a mess, my body slowly easing open and begging for more.

"Hmm, such a good boy." He chuckles. "You love this, don't you? I bet you've been biding your time secretly wanting me in this ass."

"Ah!" I scream the sting of him slapping my ass shocks me to my core. Rubbing his palm against where he just smacked, I'm humming with pleasure, my cock hard enough it'd cut steel. I don't think I've ever been this hard before in my life.

"Now, I know I'm not as big as you or pierced for that matter. But having a cock lodged into your ass, it can feel weird and different. Especially being your first time, but if it ever becomes too much, tell me. You control this, you con–"

"I'm not made of glass, Gabriel, just do it. I can't–AH–*shit.*"

Gabriel chuckles, the tip of his cock pressing against my hole. There's the faint sound of a bottle of lube opening a cool sensation nearly overcoming the burning of my ass being torn in half. Gabriel isn't large, not saying he's small, his dick fits him. But the way he's pressed against me might as well be a ten-inch-wide pole being shoved into me.

"Breathe baby, breathe," Gabriel soothes, rubbing his palm against my dick which was slowly softening. But the moment my man touches me, I'm hot on fire. Ready for anything he throws my way. "That's it, love, such a good boy. Fuck, oh love," he murmurs. "Bare down, baby, my tip is in and that was the worst of it. You're spread wide for me now."

I nod, my eyes beginning to water. I can't even remember the last time I cried, but between his cock slowly rocking into me, and his hot and wet hand stroking my cock, I'm losing all types of feelings, and everything is becoming one.

"Gabriel," I hiss, my body breaking out in shivers.

"It's okay, baby, you did it."

Snapping my eyes open, I'm immediately hit with the sight of his hand wrapped around me. I groan at the sight, but when my eyes snag to his cock lodged into my ass, everything fades away. And while it burns, and the dull ache is there, I need him to move. I need him to own me and love me.

"Move, Little Rabbit." My voice comes out husky and for fucks sake I'm obsessed. Only Gabriel could bring me to my knees. Only him.

"You're so fucking tight, my love. Fuck, you're so warm." He shudders, pressing a kiss against my inner thigh. Letting go of the comforter, I can't keep my hands off him. Pulling up, I hiss when his dick presses that sweet spot inside me. I ignore it the best I can before grabbing the back of his neck and dragging him towards me.

"Fuck me, Gabriel. Own me, fuck me, and own everything that I am," I whisper against his lips. "Don't be gentle with me. Wreck me, ruin me, steal everything that I am."

Gabriel's eyes darken, his hips moving back before snapping forward. Wrecking my ass in the best way, he rocks into me, faster and harder. His eyes never stray. Always on me. Our skin slaps together, my ass milking his cock. And when his hand snakes down between us and wraps around my leaking and pulsing dick I nearly shoot right then.

"*Fuck,*" I gasp. My mouth opens on a silent scream. Giving Gabriel access, he thrusts his tongue into my mouth. Claiming and owning, his obsession pours out as he pounds into me.

"I'm going to cum," he mutters against my mouth. My hands grab his hips, willing him to stay in me. "Tobias, I'm–fuck..." he hisses, biting down on my bottom lip.

"Cum, cum in me, Little Rabbit." My fingers digging into his ass, I refuse to let him pull out of me. Even if I have to overpower him, I'm becoming a needy cum slut for him. "Mark me, make me yours, own my ass the only wAYYY!" Cum shoots from my cock, spraying against his stomach.

"Fu–*fuckkkkkk.*" Gabriel's hips jerk, his eyes slamming shut as he buries his tongue into my mouth. I can feel his hot cum soaking my hole, possessing me. Gabriel falls against my chest, his dick slipping from me.

"Tobias," he whispers against my neck, pressing his lips against my vein. "Fuck."

"You swear too much." I chuckle, wrapping my arms around his back, my legs stretching out. I groan, the feeling I had lost in my legs coming back.

"You love it."

Nodding my head, I kiss the side of his face, breathing him in. I smile when Gabriel doesn't say anything, only his snores filling the air.

23

Gabriel

"**I**'m home, bitches!" someone screams. Bolting up, my hand presses against my chest, searching around for who just screamed at the top of their lungs. Only the room is empty, besides Tobias lying next to me on his stomach.

"Tobias?" I mumble, reaching over to shake him awake. "Tobias!" I growl, shaking him harder.

"Leave me alone!" he hisses, flopping his head to the other side, ignoring me.

Biting my lip, I debate on it for two seconds before I reach over and twist his nipple, and for good measure, I yank.

"OW, FUckkk. Okay, I'm awake." Tobias shoves my hand off him. Twisting to lie on his back, he holds his injured nipple while staring daggers at me.

I open my mouth to tell him about the stranger in the house, never getting the chance before someone pounds on the door. "Tobias, wake the fuck up!" the same feminine voice calls through the door.

"Oh, shit," he mutters, eyes snapping to the door.

"Who's that?" I ask with venom dripping from my voice. Jealousy courses through my veins. After everything, everything that's just happened, Tobias has one of his whores here.

"It's not what you think, Little Rabbit," he says, swinging his legs off the side.

"Yeah, and what am I supposed to think?" I ask, following him into the bathroom.

Tobias rolls his eyes, fishing out his toothbrush. Giving him the perfect opportunity to ignore me and come up with some plan. That's not for me. Narrowing my eyes at him, I spin around on my heel, snatching up my sweatpants.

"Fine, you won't tell me, guess I'll just figure it out for myself," I yell, throwing the door open. I don't see anyone, but that's fine. It gives me more time to fuel this anger bubbling inside. Because fuck Tobias if that's what he's about. I'm not going to just stand here and let him walk all over me, let him fuck around when he said we were dating.

"Gabriel! Wait up!" he yells after me.

"Fuck you," I spit, racing down the stairs. I hear faint laughter in the kitchen. *Fucking bitch.* Squaring my shoulders, I march into the kitchen, finding Zane leaning against the counter watching Salem and some chick giggle like a pair of besties.

"Gabriel!" Tobias yells behind me. Only I'm not having any of it, especially when the three in the kitchen turn and stare at me.

"Oh, wonderful, you must be Gabriel!" the girl says, throwing her wavy chocolate hair over her shoulder.

"I told you to wait up." Tobias finally catches up to me in the kitchen, standing by my side.

"Is this what you normally like? Brown hair, short females? Is this what you meant when you said you weren't gay?" I snap, pointing directly at the newcomer.

"Let me ex–"

"I don't want you to fucking explain to me about your girlfriend. I don't want to hear about it!" I yell, tears threatening to let loose. "I want to go home," I declare. I don't care if someone is after me. Fuck, let them kill me. If it puts me out of my damn misery, then let it.

"Ew." The girl gags.

"Blake, shut it!" Tobias growls, not daring to look away from me.

"Dude, it's disgusting!" She laughs. I can feel her moving towards me, not stopping until she's standing next to Tobias who's fuming. I don't know what for. I mean, he's the one who has his–

"If you don't shut your mouth right now, I'm going to tell Dad and Mom all about that time you got so drunk–"

"Okay, okay, okay," Blake snaps, waving her hand to stop him from talking. "Fucking tattletale." Muttering under her breath she backs off.

"Mom...and Dad?" I nervously bite on my bottom lip again. I swear that thing is going to fall off from how much I bite and destroy it.

"Yes, Gabriel. If you had waited two seconds for me to brush my teeth, I could have easily told you that," pointing over to Blake, "is my very annoying little sister Blake."

Peeking over at her, Blake smiles brightly at me. "Hello!"

"Uh, hello," I mumble, feeling more and more like a dumb ass. "I'm sorry." I step forward to Tobias, hoping with all these people standing around he will understand.

"We'll talk about it later." He sighs, grabbing my waist and pulling me against his chest. Yanking my head to his, he brushes his lips against mine before plunging his tongue into my mouth. I groan at the taste of him. He didn't brush his teeth, and though it sounds gross, it's him.

"Again, disgusting!" Blake gags, before laughing.

Blushing up at Tobias, I smile all for two seconds before I jump nearly three feet in the air when I notice someone else in the corner.

"Oh, don't bother with him, that's Henry, my bodyguard," Blake says, shoving food into her mouth.

Nodding my head, I glance around the room, Zane with his murderous look, and Salem smiling while pouring flour into a baking dish. For once, my mind is at ease, feeling content and like I belong.

I groan when Tobias shifts. "Little Rabbit," he whispers into my ear, my body sliding off his.

"Where are you going?" I mumble, my face now buried in the pillow.

"Kyler texted. He said he found some information, and we're meeting up a few hours away. I'll be back, Little Rabbit," Tobias mumbles, biting lightly on my earlobe. Groaning, I twist my head, capturing his mouth with mine.

"Come back to me," I mutter, sleep pulling me back under.

"Always." I barely catch what he says before I fall into a deep sleep.

I was asleep for thirty minutes before the dull ache in my chest woke me up, the unsettling feeling creeping along my heart, pounding, and no matter how much I tried to calm down nothing worked. I shower, changing my clothes four different times before I settle for a pair of joggers and one of Tobias's sweatshirts. Usually, his scent, his things, calm me down.

This doesn't work.

I pace around the bedroom, trying to reason with myself, yet that doesn't even work. The only thing besides Tobias that has ever worked was donuts. And I know he keeps a supply for me. Climbing down the stairs, I make my way into the kitchen, pulling the glazed donuts down from the cabinet. Shoving half the thing into my mouth, movement catches my eyes. Slowly making my way to the back porch, I notice Blake standing outside, her arms crossed over her chest. Pulling the door open, I step out into the cold air, almost debating on running back inside where it's warm. Even in December, the south is cold.

"Hey," I say, closing the door behind me.

"Somethings wrong," Blake says, not glancing in my direction.

Nervously looking where she is, I don't see anything, just pitch black, the wind whipping around our heads.

"Wh–what do you mean?" I ask, my fingers itching for the phone that I so conveniently left upstairs.

"Emilia pinged Kyler's phone, and he's still in the city. The warehouse Tobias was talking about isn't in the city. It's two hours west, on an abandoned road. Nothing important happens at that warehouse. I tried calling him but there's no answer."

Nodding my head, I try to understand what she was talking about, but I was never good at reading between the lines. I need a clear picture, plain words.

"Either he's under attack or we are." She sighs, digging her nails into her arms, her knuckles turning white.

"What makes you say that?" I ask, trying to keep my voice calm. I don't need the Mafia princess thinking I'm terrified when she's not.

"We can't reach Tobias," she states.

"But w–we're safe. I mean we're with an enforcer and a-a, I'm not sure what Salem is, but I know others in your world are scared of her." My breathing picks up, bile rising in my throat. I can't be going through this again. It's been fifteen years. I'm safe; I'm not involved in this.

"They're not here. It's just us."

"What?" I yell. "Wh–where did they go?"

"Zane went with Tobias for backup, so even if they were under attack, they'd be fine. Kyler and Zane together would make anyone piss themselves. Kyler alone is scary enough. And Salem is with Aziza down the road, I think."

"You think?" I screech.

Blake's side-eyes me. "I'm barely seventeen, what do you want from me?"

Right on cue, the lights from inside go out. The heater from inside that you could hear outside goes out. I can't see anything. Blake becomes a blur, and when I feel a hand grab at me, my body screams at me to fight.

"Come on," Blake growls, tightening her grip on me.

"Uh, y–yeah." I'm at a loss on what to do. Instead, I follow the child like I'm not a thirty-year-old man.

Blake drags us towards the house, ripping the door open just as the sound of bullets exploding near us goes off. Suddenly Blake is thrown back, screaming at the top of her lungs.

"Henry!" I yell, remembering her personal bodyguard is here.

"H–he–fuck," Blake cries out. Taking a step forward, I reach out to where I think she fell, my foot knocking into something. "DON'T STEP ON ME!" she screams.

"Shit, sorry," I whisper, getting to my knees. My eyes slowly adjust to the dark, taking in Blake's small frame lying on the ground holding her arm. "Ohmygod, ohmygod." I'm full of panic, my heart beating too fast inside my chest. I can't breathe.

"Gabriel..." Blake hisses. "Look at me!" she yells, forcing my eyes to snap to hers. Fuck if she doesn't have the same attitude Tobias has. "Salem has guns everywhere in this house, find one."

Nodding my head, I stand on shaky legs, my eyes glued to the ground. Blood seeps down Blake's shoulder, down her arm onto the ground.

"Gabriel!"

Right, get a gun.

Backing away, I stumble into the kitchen, realizing I have no idea where to even look for a hidden gun.

"Check under the kitchen table, I know for sure she has one under there," I faintly hear Blake say behind me. Nodding, even though she can't see me, I trace the wall leading into the kitchen, when all of a sudden, a man stands directly in front of me. I don't get a chance to scream, yell, or even blink before I'm punched in the face. My body knocks back, the air from my lungs escapes, and three kicks hit my side.

"S—stop," Blake screams.

"Zatknis', suka," The man above me spits at her, turning his attention back to me. "Glupaya chertova shlyukha. Chertov boss, dazhe ne mogu ponyat', chto on vidit v tvoyey kiske, zadnitse."

I can't understand what he's saying. I try to wiggle away from him, but the kicks keep coming, men laughing in the distance, and worse of all this feels all too familiar.

"Dostatochno." Another man steps into view, blocking Blake from my gaze.

"Boris, chto ty delayesh'?" Blake's voice breaking through.

Blinking up, it finally dawns on me that Henry is standing over me. And he's not stopping the man from kicking me, nor is he making an attempt to do his job. He's not helping Blake who's been shot.

"Something I should've done a long time ago." He laughs, moments before something smashes into my head, darkness pulling me under.

24

Tobias

*T*here's nothing here.

The words repeat in my head. The warehouse sits empty, no prisoner that Kyler said he had. And no Kyler. Absolutely nothing. I have the gut-wrenching feeling that something is obviously wrong, but I can't put my finger on what it is.

"Tobias, there's nothing here," Zane's monotone fills my head. He's right, there's nothing here and I can't figure out why Kyler would text me saying there was a problem at this warehouse.

Pulling my phone out, I dial Kyler, my foot tapping against the gravel in irritation that he isn't going to answer when he finally does. Only it isn't his voice. A female answers.

"Hello."

"Who are you?" I growled. My eyes train on Zane who immediately picks up on my tone.

"Who are you?" she asks shyly.

"I don't have time for this, where is Kyler?" I ask, hand clenching the phone. I'm surprised I haven't broken it.

"Damn, you're grouchy," she mutters, before yelling for Kyler. There is a faint wrestling of the phone before Kyler's heavy breathing fills the line.

"What's up?"

"Seriously? That's all you have to say to me. Where the fuck are you?" I ask, switching from English to Russian.

"Dude, I'm in the city, where else would I be?" He chuckles.

"So, you're saying you didn't text me saying to meet two hours west of Salem's house at some warehouse because you found something?"

"Tobias, I didn't text you." He suddenly becomes serious.

"I... I, fuck," I mutter, confusion sinking into my gut.

"When did you get this text?" he asks, before a faint whisper of, "did you text someone off my phone?"

I want to murder him for just leaving his phone around for some random girl to get the chance to go through it. But I don't, hearing the faint mumble of her voice, but I can't make out what she's saying.

"Tobias, none of us sent a text. What's going on?"

"I got a text from you, but I guess not you, and I'm not su–"

"Fuck!" Zane growls, marching towards me, phone thrust into my face. Backing away, I squint my eyes trying to focus on what he's showing me.

"Zane, I... I don't know what I'm looking at."

"Someone tripped the security at Salem's." Ripping his phone away, he takes it away before bringing it to his ear. "Fuck," he hisses, tapping away at his phone again. "Get in the car, Tobias," he orders. Biting down on my lip, I ignore the temptation to tell him I'm technically his boss but stop when the moment I shut the door he's peeling out of the makeshift gravel driveway.

"Put me on speaker," Kyler says with the faint hint of doors opening and closing. Doing as he says, I pull up Gabriel's contact, shooting a text off.

"What's going on, Zane?" he asks before I can.

"Salem is crazy. She has so much security around the entire property. Basically, someone tripped the system, and I can't get in touch with her or Killian."

My fingers are moving before Zane finishes talking, Kyler forgotten on the other line. Gabriel's name hangs on my screen. *Hi, you've reached Gabriel. I can't–*

"No," I mutter, not believing it for one second. Gabriel has to be asleep; he can't be hurt. He's safe. Salem's house is the safest.

Hi, you've reached Gabriel–

"Tobias, what's happening?" Zane asks, his voice too steady for my liking, but I can't stop, my finger pressing the call button over again, only to get his voicemail. That gut feeling hits me, bile rising in my throat. I can't lose him, I can't. I only just found him; we've never spent any time together. I haven't shown him Russia, I haven't shown him all his artwork I hung up in our house. I haven't shown him the world.

"I–I can't reach him, Zane. He's not answering. Why isn't he answering, Za–Zane." My voice cracks, my finger continually hitting the call button though I know exactly what's going to happen.

Voicemail.

"Grab my phone, call Zion."

Doing as he says, my hands shake as I pull this Zion's contact up.

"Speaker."

Pressing the button, a deep growling voice answer, "What?"

"We have an issue," Zane says, racing down the street, hitting the highway. Tears fill my eyes, blinding me from being able to see.

"I don't care," he answers, and I nearly scream at him until Zane shakes his head.

"Where's Izel?"

My head snaps up at the mention of that name. I know that name. "Why?"

"For fucks sake, Zion, get Izel, it's about Gabriel!" Zane bellows.

My eyes drop down to my phone, the picture of Gabriel sleeping on my chest, the picture I took just last night when he had fallen asleep on me. I want to take the last few hours back; I want to ignore that text that Kyler hadn't sent. To go back to sleeping with Gabriel wrapped around me.

"Zane?" a female voice appears, assuming it's Izel. "What's going on?"

Zane looks at me, nodding towards the phone. Obviously wanting me to take over. Except I can't. If this is his sister, this isn't how I want to meet her. Gabriel says she is the nicest person, always forgiving, but she won't forgive me for this. If something happens to Gabriel, I won't survive, I couldn't.

"Tell me, tell me what is going on? What happened? Where's Gabriel!" Izel's voice shakes, her breathing picking up.

"I can't reach him," I mutter, barely moving an inch, my body melting into the seat.

"I, I don't understand. What do you mean? What do you mean you can't reach him? Who are you?"

Zane waits for me to say something, but I can't. The tears fall down my cheeks. I'm supposed to be the strong Pakhan, the one that takes over for my father, a ruthless killer. But I'm weak, I've always been weak, and now that Gabriel is involved, I'm nothing but a mess.

"Someone better start talking," Zion growls into the phone.

"Tobias got a text from his enforcer that he found who had been threatening Gabriel and to meet him a few hours west from Salem's. I went with him for backup, leaving Gabriel and Blake–"

"Who's Blake?"

"Tobias's sister, and her bodyguard Henry. They were all at Salem's."

"Fucking bitch," Zion mutters under his breath, not caring that we can clearly hear him.

"Watch your mouth when you talk about my wife," Zane snaps, his knuckles whitening on the steering wheel.

"Anyway, we got to the location, no Kyler, nothing... It was a trap to get us away from the house and now we can't reach Blake, Salem, Gabriel, or Henry. No one is answering, and the security was tripped."

It was deadly quiet, no one speaking, no one breathing. I looked down to make sure they hadn't hung up.

"Aziza's working on their location, Killian is on the phone with Dimitri, who's on their plane heading here... Gabriel's phone is pinging at the house, but uh... fuck–"

"What? Just tell me, tell me!" I scream, the air from my lungs escaping when Zion says, "They knew he had a tracker. They knew somehow and cut it out. It's down the road from Salem's, which means they left."

"How can you tell they cut it out?" Zane asks as I wrap my brain around the fact Gabriel has a tracker or did have a tracker in him.

"Aziza designed it. It pings when it's no longer in use, or well, in humans. It was in his hand, and now it's not."

I have so many questions, like how do they know each other? How did Aziza get brought into this, and how did Gabriel get wrapped into all this? He's normal, and he isn't involved in the Mafia. Sure, I don't know much about his family. Emilia could never get any information on him, someone had wiped any trace of his existence from the web.

"Why couldn't I find anything on him?" I blurt out.

"Aziza wiped mine and his identity from everything. Kind of like what she did for Salem." Izel's muffled cries ring in my ears.

Nodding my head, even though they can't see or hear me, it makes sense. I just don't understand how Aziza is involved in any of this.

"Remember when Aunt Aziza was kidnapped when you were little?" Zane must have picked up on my confusion.

"Somewhat. I mean, I remember everything that happened with Aunt Salem, her being in the hospital, the accident with Aunt Aziza, but then... I mean, I was kept in the dark, mostly. I vaguely remember hearing about Aziza missing with Uncle Killian until we were all at the hospital again when she was found..." I mutter. I mean I was seven. Sure, I should remember more about that time, but my parents kept us in the dark for the most part. Mom didn't want the darkness of the world to touch us yet.

"Fuck... okay, uh well, Zion and Aziza and Killian are all childhood friends. When Aziza had been kidnapped after Killian and her ran away, uh... well, Izel was there and helped get her out before Killian asked Zion to go get her out of the house."

"I'm so confused." I shake my head. None of what Zane is saying makes sense. Childhood friends? Izel being kidnapped and locked in a house?

"I'm explaining this bad; I don't know much. I mean at this point Salem, and I were focused on ourselves. We weren't involved in whatever Zion did."

"As it should be," Zion says, not caring what comes from his mouth.

"Alright, listen, meet us at Salem's house. Dimitri and Mila will be landing in the next hour. We're about an hour out, and we'll figure out where Salem and everyone is."

Everyone says their goodbyes, but all I can focus on is the fact that Gabriel can't fight. Salem can hold her own, she's smart. Blake, as much as she is a pain in the ass, she's a Mafia princess, she knows this. She knows how to work a gun; she's killed someone before for fucks sake. But Gabriel, my poor, innocent Gabriel.

I'm not going to survive without him.

Gabriel

F our hours.

240 minutes.

14,400 seconds.

My body shakes against the wall, freezing as my bare skin is exposed to the frigid air. I can't see two feet in front of me, but none of this is new. It's the same as it was fifteen years ago, only it's a different set of monsters. These monsters are connected to Blake, and I was in the way. They wanted her, and I just happened to be there.

The darkness surrounds me, pulling me under, reminding me that I'm not human. Reminding me I'm meant for nothing but pain and torture. The coldness wraps around me, sinking me into the dark part of my head. The place I was promised I'd never have to visit again. No amount of therapy was going to fix this. We're never going to be saved, and when I hear Blake's scream, I cover my ears, the tears streaming down. I knew what they were doing to her. I've lived this once before. I've been here before; this was nothing new. Only instead of my sister being on the other side, it was Tobias' sister. The Bratva princess.

Only I hope they kill her quickly. No one deserves to live with this kind of pain.

Six hours

360 minutes

21,600 seconds

Blake lays her head in my lap, blinking. We're aware of our surroundings, but neither of us are alert. Her body shakes, as she shoves her fingers into her mouth. I'm not sure why. I want to ask, but I can't. She hasn't spoken since they brought her out, and I think around the five-hour mark, she stopped screaming. I thought she was dead when they dragged her into this tiny closet, dropping her body like a bag of bones. She barely registered when I pulled her onto my lap. She didn't make a sound, and what scared me the most was the vacant expression she wore.

I hum low in my throat, trying to bring some type of calmness, but it worries me more that she's so damn quiet. Not a peep, nothing but shallow breaths. It's the only thing that brings me some peace.

And when one of them opens the door, his evil smile peeks down at us. He yanks Blake by her arm, and she doesn't fight him, doesn't move.

"Let her go!" I scream, pushing off the ground. I don't make it two inches before something hits me in the face, darkness pulling me under again.

26

—◆—

Tobias

Zion and Zane glare at each other.

Izel, Salem, Aziza, and my mom all huddle together, Salem trying to calm my mom down while Aziza holds Izel.

Killian types away on his computer while my father barks orders at some of his guards. Everything blurs together.

I stand there, my eyes glued to the blood pool in the middle of the kitchen. No one had bothered to clean it up, and my throat tightens. It's either Blake's or Gabriel's, and I wish it was neither. I can't lose Gabriel. Not when I finally got him. And I can't lose my baby sister. I remember when Mom gave birth to her, and I held her for the first time. She was so tiny, but I swear when she smiled at me, I knew what sibling love was. She is the most annoying person, but always has my back.

"Tobias." Someone calls me, but I can't focus on anything. I shouldn't have left Gabriel alone. I should have listened to Kyler when he said to leave him alone. I should have listened.

"Tobias!"

Snapping my head up, Zion is now hovering over me like the fucking beast that he is, his black skull mask firmly in place. Which is another thing I learned. Apparently, Zion is The Butcher, the famously hired hitman. Rumor was he retired, which was true, only because he found love. In Izel, whose brother is the love of my life.

I love him.

The thought hits me out of nowhere. But is it really from nowhere? I knew I had feelings for him for a while. I just don't understand why I never told him.

"Pup." Izel sighs, coming to sit next to me. "You're Tobias."

Nodding my head, I stare down at my lap, feeling like a failure. I lost her brother, her wonderful brother whom she did everything to protect. And I blew it. I let him get taken.

"Can I tell you something about my baby brother?" she asks, taking my hand in hers. There is a faint sound of Zion growling, but Izel shakes her head, causing him to shut up.

"Sure," I mumble.

"When he was thirteen, I found him crying in the closet with all these stuffed animals. He was hiding, and when I finally convinced him to talk to me, it was hours by the way, I had tried to crack a joke about finally coming out of the closet. Little did I know, when he said he was scared I was going to look at him differently, I had no idea what he was talking about until it finally clicked. We both cried and when

I promised him that his secret was safe with me, we both declared when we finally made it out that we were going to find partners that understood our past. For me, I needed someone who knew that touch was a hard thing. I was raped and beaten since I was thirteen. I needed someone who would push me but also let me be my crazy natural self. Which Zion does, he lays with me–"

"Red," Zion growls, his dark eyes narrowing at her. Only instead of anger, all I see is love.

"He doesn't like people knowing he has a soft side," she whispers, "but that's what I'm trying to get to. Gabriel said he wanted someone who understood his art, and understood that he didn't want to hide in the closet again. He had been held behind a door his whole life, and he wanted someone who accepted his donuts obsession, his iced coffee addiction, and most of all understood the trust issues we carry. So, know that if Gabriel trusted you enough to know that you'd protect him, it means a lot. And he knows you're going to save him."

I didn't realize I was crying again until she leaned across, wiping a tear from my cheek. "Don't be so hard on yourself. We'll get him...and if we don't..." Glancing up, Izel gets to her feet, holding onto Zion's hand. "I'll kill you."

I swallow the lump in my throat. Knowing full well I'd let her.

"Found them." I barely register Killian speaking before I'm on my feet.

"Where?" I growl. Because whoever has them, they better know I'm not stopping until I kill. Every. Last. One. Of. Them.

The cold wind wraps around us as we cover the ground, our guns drawn. Salem stayed back with Mom, Aziza, and Izel, not knowing if this was another trap or not. Zion and Zane, as much as they hate each other, work swiftly and quickly around the building. Kyler stays close to me while my father and Killian flank behind us.

"Stay alert," Killian says into our earpieces.

The old house is barely holding together, with yellow and red graffiti and glass bottles dumped on the ground. And when Zion double clicks the earpiece, making it known it is game time, we throw the doors open. A few men who I have no idea didn't know we were right outside, barely register all of us flooding in. Zane and Zion both take them out. Stepping over their dead bodies, we continue making our way through the hallway, Zion and Zane checking each room, while Kyler and I continue on.

"Mierda!" Someone scrambles to get their gun out. Being a little rusty on my Spanish, I take aim with a bullet through the eyes.

Suddenly everything begins to happen too fast. Men pour out of the room, guns drawn, and shots ring out around us. Someone body slams me into one room, nearly missing a used needle. I roll and kick the fucker who tackled me.

"Shit," I mutter. I can't remember the last time someone got the upper hand on me. And the fucker barely flinches when I kick him in the nuts. "What the–"

A hand wraps around his forehead, a knife slicing into his throat before his body is shoved to the side. His blood coats my face, as Kyler reaches down helping me to my feet "Come on."

Checking my magazine, we check our surroundings. Zion and Zane come out of a room, and Killian and Dad both take a shot at someone before nodding their heads to continue. Coming to a set of stairs, Zion orders, "Dimitri, Killian, and I will take upstairs, you three take the basement," leaving no room for argument.

Eyes glued, we make our way down, Zion in front, Kyler behind me. The basement feels cold, and before we can register anything happening, someone tackles Zion, and a knife flies through the air slamming into Kyler's shoulder.

"FUCK!" he screams, ripping the knife out. Aiming, I shoot the bastard in the gut, watching him fall to the ground. Zion grunts. Looking over, I see him slam the fuckers head into the ground. Getting to his feet, Zion mutters, "I'm getting too old for this shit."

"Yeah, you are, Grandpa," Kyler says under his breath, earning him a scowl from the hitman.

"Come on," Zion says.

The basement is mostly open except for a few doors. Zion and Kyler begin opening doors while I stand there, spinning in circles at where he could be, where they could be, and when I hear something behind the last door, Zion and Kyler both look at me before reaching for the door.

It's as if they slowly open the door, and my life flashes before my eyes. Gabriel sits there fully naked, while my sister lays next to him facing away. Covered in blood.

"Fuck." Zion rips his coat off, reaching forward.

"NO!" Gabriel screams, grabbing Blake and pulling her towards him. "Don't TOUCH HER, DON'T TOUCH HER!"

Dad, Zane, and Killian come running in. My breath rises as I'm unsure what to do, knowing we should have brought one of the girls to deal with this. Because glancing around, we have no idea how to handle this.

"Little Rabbit," I mumble, pushing my way through until I'm in the doorway of the small closet. My breath hitches as his wild eyes snap to me, uncertain if he knows it was me or not. "Little Rabbit, it's me. It's me, baby." My voice cracks, my hand reaching out. I think he's going to smack me away but when a tear slips down his cheek, I know he's back.

"Here." Zion passes me the coat. Laying it over Blake, I kneel further in.

"Little Rabbit, let me take her. It's okay, it's me, let me take my sister." My voice cracks even more. I can barely hold it together. Gabriel slowly lets go of his death grip on her, letting me carefully scoop her up. I barely have time to move before Zane bends down, picking her up.

"Come on, love, come on," I mumble, reaching in for Gabriel.

"Tobias?" Gabriel mumbles, and when I nod, he flings himself into my arms, crying. I catch him falling back against the ground.

"Little Rabbit, I got you. I have you," I choke out, my arms wrapping around him. Trying my best to sit up, I move him around keeping him firmly around me as I get to my feet.

"Here," My father says, handing me his coat. Glancing over I take it in one hand as Gabriel digs his heels into my ass and fingers into my neck.

"Thank you," I mutter.

"Come on, let's get out of here before anyone else comes back," Dad says.

Squeezing Gabriel, we turn just as the sound of a gun cocking and an unfamiliar voice fills the air. "I can't let you do that."

My body freezes. Gabriel whimpers and that's all I need to know. Whoever this fucker is, his greasy gray hair sticks up everywhere, and his crazed eyes lock onto mine.

"Who are you?" Dad asks, going to stand in front of me.

"Don't move." Another voice feels the air, coming out of nowhere. Henry. I don't even get to question what he's doing and why he's not trying to save Blake when it dawns on me.

"He's the mole," I say.

Henry smiles over at me, taking his place next to the stranger, both of them with their guns raised. In a normal throwdown, I wouldn't care. I would shoot them even with the chances someone would get hit. But with Blake in Zane's arms and Gabriel shivering in mine, I can't.

"Mole?" Dad questions, not looking away from them.

"Billy and Nathan, we found them making a deal with the cartel. We killed them both before we could find out how they knew about our shipments. We were looking for who the mole could be... I thought they worked under me," I answer, glaring at Henry, hatred filling my every fiber. "Gabriel, get behind me," I whisper into his ear.

Gabriel slowly slides down, getting behind me. I widen my stance, trying to make him invisible behind me.

"Why, Henry?" Dad asks, his feet moving to the left just a tad bit.

"Why? WHY? Because I'm tired of taking orders from a fourteen-year-old girl who walks all over her father who's weak!" One thing about my father, he's not weak nor does he let Blake walk all over him. He just never beat us or forced us to abide by the typical Mafia standard.

"Enough," the other man spits. His eyes still haven't moved from me. Henry might hate Blake and my father but whoever he is, he wants me. "Drop your guns," he growls, waving his own like a madman.

No one moves. Zion stands in front of Zane blocking Blake, but his eyes linger to Gabriel who's behind me. Kyler and Killian glance at Dad to see what he wants.

"Now!" he growls.

Dad slowly lowers his gun, kicking it over to Henry. One by one each of us lowers our guns, and when I'm the last one to do so, I don't.

"I don't think so," I say, not backing down to this piece of shit that hurt my Gabriel. "Who are you? You're the one who sent someone after Gabriel; you're the one who sent me those pictures," I state. He's the only one who could have.

Slowly a smile spreads across his face. "You're right. It was fun, watching you and your disgusting whore."

I growl, narrowing my eyes. He is going to die painfully, and I am going to enjoy every second of it.

"Nah uh, don't even think about it. He fucked Billy and Nathan. Did you know that?" He laughs, and Gabriel's hands tighten against my back. I bite my inner cheek at the mention of Gabriel's ex, possibly two of them. I just didn't know it was both, and it doesn't matter. He's mine now. No one's going to touch him again.

"It didn't take long to tap into the network, trying to track his phone to find him at your dear old friend Salem's. It's a shame that she's not here. I would love to meet the famous little slut that took out the Italian—"

"Watch your mouth," Zane growls, stepping forward and bumping into Zion.

"And the old-time retired hitman...." he says, swinging his gaze to Zion. "The Butcher..."

I have no idea how he knows any of this, but I'm losing patience. Blake and Gabriel need the hospital. I need to tell Izel her brother made it and hope that Zion doesn't kill me in the end.

"So, what's the plan, kill us all?" I ask, finding my voice rough and coarse.

"Well, yeah." He laughs. "I mean, you killed my sons. I think it's only fair I take out the beloved one of Dimitri, Russian Mafia, and I mean if I can take out more of the retired old—"

Everything happens in a flash. A knife comes flying out, impaling Henry in the throat. All hell breaks loose. Everyone jumps for their guns, Zane shielding Blake with his body, and I backing Gabriel against the wall. My fingers reach for my gun, just as the crack of gunshots rings out. My ears ring, my body ignites, my stomach rolls. Billy and Nathan's father lie on the ground, gasping for air, Henry dead on the floor.

Swinging around, I lock eyes with Gabriel. His breath comes in ragged, my eyes searching to see where he's hit. "Fuck," I mutter. I don't see anything, only him standing with my father's coat wrapped around his body. He's safe.

He's okay...He's sa...

Breathing becomes painful, sweat beading at my forehead. I hear movement around me, but I can only see Gabriel. I only want to see him. My vision blurs. I'm not sure what's happening, not when my knees buckle, and I go down like a sack of shit again. The last thing I hear is Gabriel screaming my name.

27

Gabriel

3 weeks later

"Hey."

I look up from my sketchbook as Dimitri makes his way into the hospital room. I bite my bottom lip, worried today will be the day he will kick me out. It hasn't happened yet, but there was no telling with him.

"Hello," I mutter, sitting up, clenching my artwork to my chest. *Please don't make me leave. Please don't.*

"Nurse told me you've been here all night again," he says, walking in towards Tobias.

I nod my head, even though he's not paying attention to me. I've been here every night for the past three weeks since he was shot. Three long weeks of me sketching Tobias over and over again, never getting it right. And nighttime is when I break apart. It's when his family goes home and I'm alone.

"They tell me you refuse to leave his side," he states, blinking over at me.

"I won't." I don't know where I find my voice but I can't leave him.

Dimitri nods his head, glancing at his son before looking at me again. I squirm under his gaze. I'm the whole reason his son is in here. He never would have been in the basement looking for me or in this hospital if it weren't for me.

"You love him?" he asks.

"Yes." Because I do. I never got to tell him, and the fact I never got to whisper those words to him, it kills me.

"He'll come back to you. He's a stubborn man, Gabriel. He'll come back," Dimitri mumbles before heading back to the door. I think he's going to say something, but instead, he shakes his head, opens the door, and shuts it behind him.

Pulling my knees to my chest, my watery eyes drop back to my love, lying in the hospital bed, Tubes running out of his body, a tube down his throat, and worst of all a ventilator being the only thing keeping him alive.

28

Tobias

3 weeks later

B *eep.*
Beep.
Beep.

The constant beeping shakes me awake, and I reach for whatever the fuck it is to shut the thing up. My side pitches in pain the moment I raise my hand. Fuck, even wiggling my finger causes my body to shake with pain.

What the fuck... what happened—Gabriel.

My eyes pop open, brightness blinding me for a moment before someone grabs my shoulder. "It's okay, calm down," their soft voice whispers to the pounding in my head. "Pup, can you go get him?"

Blinking the blurriness away, I meet Izel's gaze looking at me. "Glad to see you awake, finally." She smiles brightly, patting my shoulder before easing back.

"I...what..." My throat burns, sandpaper rubbing against my windpipe. I blink, trying to recall what happened.

"It... it was a whole mess," she whispers. "The only important thing is you're alive."

The door slams open, ringing echoes around my ear, but the moment I see his pale blue eyes, his messy, a little longer than usual, shaggy hair, it's the only thing that matters. Gabriel. My Little Rabbit.

He chokes on a sob, biting down on his lip. I don't know what he's waiting for, but I don't like that he's standing there in the doorway, and I don't like the uncertainty in his eyes.

"Gabriel," I murmur, my voice cracking. And that's all it takes; his knees buckle as he rushes to my side. Slamming his body against mine, I grunt in pain, but refuse to let him move. My Gabriel. Questions swarm around, needing answers to what happened. Where is everyone else? Who else was hurt? But none of those matters, not with him in my arms. Him being my only focus.

"To—"

"Shh, it's okay," I tell him, kissing the side of his head.

"I thought I lost you." He sobs, clenching harder to my gown.

"I'm here, I'm right here, Little Rabbit." My own tears leak down my cheeks, my fingers running underneath his shirt, needing to feel him against me, even if it's painful. "I'm not going anywhere."

Gabriel lays his face in my neck, his snores the only thing keeping me calm. After our little crying fest, my doctor came in and gave me the usual run-down. And the little fact that I've been in a coma for the past six weeks.

"He stayed with you the entire time," Dad mutters from the bedside. Looking down at Gabriel, I kiss his head the best way I can without straining or ripping my stitches. "We going to talk about it?"

Glaring up at my father, I'm unsure what to say. I knew this conversation was going to have to happen. I wasn't willing to let him go. But I didn't think about how I would actually approach this conversation.

"Tobias, you might have my temper, but you've got your mother's love. I can see it all over your face, so don't even try to bullshit me." Dad sighs, leaning back.

"I love him," I breathe. I haven't told him that yet, but saying it out loud for the first time, I don't want to stop. "I love him, and I won't leave him."

Dad sighs again. I hate when he does that. And the same expression when he's thinking is usually never good.

"Just spit it out," I growl, causing Gabriel to shift and tighten his hold he has on my gown.

"When I found your mother, I tried to stay away. I mean, we saved her from the crate they were moving, and instead of taking her to the hospital, I simply just took her, knowing how wrong it was. But in my head, I wanted her and would do anything to prove to her that she would be better with me than anyone else."

I have no idea where he's going with this and even with me frowning Dad continues on.

"I watched her grow and become the woman I began to love, and when we got pregnant with you, I didn't think I could love her even more. But I did, and every day I fall a little more in love with her than before. I can't breathe without her. She's on my mind every second of every day, even when she's next to me. I have this burning pas—"

"Dad," I groan, not needing to hear about his burning passion for my mother. It's gross and so wrong.

"You feel the same for him. You blocked him from being shot. Salem showed up, saving us all once again," he growls, rolling his eyes. I chuckle, knowing damn well he hates Salem always saving his ass. "Henry died. Todd, the boy's father, on the other hand... Well, he took a while to die. Zion, Zane, and Kyler had a fun bonding experience with that one."

Nodding my head, I search trying to remember the events, but it's all a blur.

"Gabriel was a mess and wouldn't leave your side. He sleep, let's say he had a mouthful to say about letting you live. Something he read about online, he said. Something about the Mafia not accepting those who love the same sex..."

I open my mouth to defend Gabriel only Dad waves a hand stopping me.

"I don't care. I don't care if you like pussy or cock." Way to go, Dad. "You can't help who you love, as long as you treat them well and they do the same. I don't care, they just have to know what being involved with you means."

"He does," I state. I'm not sure if he actually does, but I will help him. I will support Gabriel no matter what.

"Then I support you, Son." He smiles.

Trying not to let the emotions get the best of me, I nod, blinking down at Gabriel. My heart squeezes, feeling pride knowing he's mine. All mine.

Epilogue

I wake up to Gabriel rubbing circles against my heart.

After the talk with Dad, Gabriel woke up and told me he loves me too. He cried while telling me what he saw down in the basement and how he thought he was going to lose me. While I stay in the hospital for the following few weeks, complaining most of the time, much to my dislike, Gabriel agrees with everything the doctors and nurses tell me to do.

Dad, Mom, and Blake went back to Russia a few days ago. Blake isn't doing too well, refusing to talk, and no one can touch her without her trying to murder them. And the worst part, she looks at you like she doesn't recognize who you are. Gabriel told us he doesn't know what they did to her, only that at one point the screams stopped and she hasn't been the same.

Izel and Zion went back home, promising to visit soon. Though I'm not sure if I ever want to see Zion again. He never takes that creepy mask off, and when I question Gabriel about it, he shrugs and won't tell me what he looks like.

I still don't understand everything that happened. Gabriel struggles to tell me about it. Not that I blame him. If he were the one shot, I'd probably lose my mind. Not probably, I would.

"You ever think back to the time you broke into my apartment?" Gabriel asks, pressing his lips against my shoulder.

"Hmmm," I moan. I've been cleared for exactly one week, but Gabriel being stubborn still won't let me do anything but kiss him. I've tried giving him a blow job but ended up hissing in pain when I pushed my body too hard.

"I couldn't stop thinking about your hands," he mutters, running a hand down my chest to my stomach. "I thought about what they would feel like..."

"Gabriel."

"Let me finish..." he moans, his hand leading further down. "I thought about them wrapped around my throat, what you would feel like pressed against me."

"Fuck it," I growled, throwing my body over his, only a slight tinge of pain, but I ignore it. Doing exactly that, I wrap my hand around his throat.

"I could barely control myself when you sat there on your couch. I had too many filthy things running through my head. I wanted to choke you with my cock, but I also wanted to wrap myself around that brain of yours and find out why you were so sad."

"I was waiting for you," he murmurs, wrapping his legs around my waist.

"Well, you don't have to wait any longer," I tell him, slamming my lips against his.

Acknowledgements

First and foremost, I want to thank you the reader. Without you, I wouldn't be able to share their story. It's been a wild ride but a fun one.

Thank you to my PA, **Kaitlyn Denny**, you've helped me more than you will ever know.

Thank you to **Susan,** and **Haley** for editing and proofreading, y'all are real ones.

Thank you, **Jordan** for being an incredible friend and always believing in me, even when I don't. You're always there and always a phone call away. You're an amazing friend and saved me more than once.

Thank you, **Mom and Dad**, you always call and give me a reason to smile, especially on those sad days. (hope you love the artwork, Dad)

Thank you, **Shania** (shaniasbookshelf – Instagram) months ago you asked someone to use a line in their book. Thank you for allowing me to use it, it fits Tobias and Gabriel so well, and I'm literally obsessed.

And lastly thank you to my husband, you're always pushing me to do write and live my dream. You're my biggest supporter.

About the Author

Ryan Mundy is a twenty-five year old, living in South Carolina. But often traveling to Michigan. If she's not busy writing from the voices in her head, she's reading or rewatching shows she's obsessed with.

Keep up to date:

instagram: authorryanmundy

TikTok: @authorryanmundy

Website: https://www.ryanmundywrites.com/

For signed copies check website

Ryan Mundy xoxo

ALSO BY

<u>War Path</u>
Psychological War
Love and War
Red Obsession

<u>The Deranged</u>
Stalked
Wrecked (coming soon)
Ruined (coming soon)
Stolen (coming soon)